ABBY'S LUCKY THIRTEEN

MARTINEZ SCHOOL LIBRARY

**Other books by
Ann M. Martin**

Rachel Parker, Kindergarten Show-off
Eleven Kids, One Summer
Ma and Pa Dracula
Yours Turly, Shirley
Ten Kids, No Pets
Slam Book
Just a Summer Romance
Missing Since Monday
With You and Without You
Me and Katie (the Pest)
Stage Fright
Inside Out
Bummer Summer

BABY-SITTERS LITTLE SISTER series
THE BABY-SITTERS CLUB mysteries
THE BABY-SITTERS CLUB series

ABBY'S LUCKY THIRTEEN

Ann M. Martin

AN
APPLE
PAPERBACK

SCHOLASTIC INC.
New York Toronto London Auckland Sydney

*Special thanks to
Robin Dorman, Julie Komorn,
David Levithan, and Helen Perelman
for sharing their
Bar and Bat Mitzvah stories.*

*The author gratefully acknowledges
Nola Thacker
for her help in
preparing this manuscript.*

Cover art by Hodges Soileau

*If you purchased this book without a cover, you should be aware that this book
is stolen property. It was reported as "unsold and destroyed" to the publisher,
and neither the author nor the publisher has received any payment for this
"stripped book."*

No part of this publication may be reproduced in whole or in part,
or stored in a retrieval system, or transmitted in any form or by any
means, electronic, mechanical, photocopying, recording, or other-
wise, without written permission of the publisher. For information
regarding permission, write to Scholastic Inc., 555 Broadway, New
York, NY 10012.

ISBN 0-590-22880-3

Copyright © 1996 by Ann M. Martin. All rights reserved. Published
by Scholastic Inc. THE BABY-SITTERS CLUB, THE BABY-SITTERS
CLUB logo, APPLE PAPERBACKS, and the APPLE PAPERBACKS
logo are registered trademarks of Scholastic Inc.

12 11 10 9 8 7 6 5 4 3 2 1   6 7 8 9/9 0 1/0

Printed in the U.S.A.   40

First Scholastic printing, April 1996

CHAPTER 1

"Abby? Abby!"

I looked up from where I was sitting on the sidelines of the soccer field and grinned and waved. My twin sister, Anna, and her violin were standing there.

Well, okay, the violin wasn't standing there. My sister was holding it in its case under one arm, while she waved to me with the other.

I finished lacing up my sneaks, jammed my cleats in my pack, and stood up to join her.

Although my sister and I are twins, we are identical only in appearance. We both have deep brown eyes that are almost black; we both wear glasses or contacts (depending on our moods); we both have dark brown, thick, curly hair, and pointed chins. But Anna wears her hair shorter than mine, with bangs. And although she is coordinated, she isn't athletic. Her talent is music, and while I like to *listen* to music, I couldn't carry a tune in a bucket.

Anna is first chair in the Stoneybrook Middle School orchestra, which means she is really, really good on the violin. She also plays the piano and she's been known to do a few turns on our father's old harmonica. In fact, I bet Anna could play any instrument on earth after only a couple of tries.

Also, Anna doesn't have asthma and allergies. Life makes me sneeze. Kitty litter, dogs, dust, feather pillows, down comforters, down coats, tomatoes, shellfish, milk, and cheese all give me fits. But although I've had a couple of serious asthma attacks (which got zapped by a quick trip to the emergency room), there's no way I'm gonna let that slow me down.

I don't play the violin or the piano or the harmonica. I do my best playing with my feet. Soccer is my game, but I also like running, skiing, basketball, and softball. I love sports. Back on Long Island, where we used to live, I was the star forward, leading scorer, and co-captain of the soccer team.

I'm not bragging. In my opinion, the only people who brag are the ones who aren't first chair, if you know what I mean.

"How was band practice?" I asked Anna as I jogged up to her. I waved good-bye to my teammates on the SMS soccer team and fell into step beside my sister.

"It's the orchestra, not the band, and you

know it," said Anna, smiling at me.

"Sorry. I didn't mean to do *violins* to your feelings," I replied, making an awful pun on the word *violence*.

My sister groaned.

"Sorry. That was *viol*," I couldn't resist adding.

I like puns, the worse the better. My sister tolerates them. Another difference between us.

"If you make another *vile* pun, Abby, you're in trouble."

"Oh, fiddle," I wisecracked and ducked as Anna took a swat at me. But she was grinning.

"Practice was fine," she said. "What about yours?"

"Excellent," I said. "I love April. Perfect soccer weather. Too bad we have to go to Bat Mitzvah class. I wish . . ."

Wait, wait, wait. I'm doing what I always do. Going at top speed. And leaving you behind, right?

Here's the deal.

I'm Abby Stevenson. I'm thirteen years old and I live in Stoneybrook, Connecticut, with my only sibling, Anna, and our mother, Rachel. We moved here from Long Island not too long ago, after our mother got this great promotion at her publishing house in New York City. The promotion allowed my mother to buy a bigger house, and since she felt the family needed a change, we moved to Stoney-brook.

Neither Anna nor I was delighted with the Big Move. Although we didn't talk about it, I know we both felt that there had been enough changes in the past few years. We didn't want to leave the house where our father had lived with us, either. He was killed in a car crash when we were nine.

That was the worst time in my life. The driver of the truck who hit our father's car only broke his arm, but our father was killed instantly. For a long time, my mother wouldn't even mention his name. For a long time, I forgot how to laugh and I couldn't make jokes.

For a long time . . . no, I don't want to talk about it anymore.

Anyway, we complained, we resisted, and then what did we do? We moved of course. My mother liked her new job. My twin sister joined the band — excuse me, the orchestra — at school and started making some friends. We were both invited to join this club called the Baby-sitters Club (also known as the BSC, more about that later). Anna decided to stick to her music.

I joined the club.

The members of the club became my friends, and provided not only friendship but some pretty wild adventures *and* baby-sitting jobs that brought in very welcome extra money. I also joined the soccer team, participated in class, and avoided any major asthma attacks, except for one that sent me to the emergency room and almost cancelled my membership in the BSC (but that's another story).

In short, I adjusted. We all did. I started liking Stoneybrook for real.

And then the Bat Mitzvah (pronounced *Baht Mitz-vah*) business creeps up and bites me on the ankle.

Okay, okay, a Bat Mitzvah can't bite you on the ankle. Becoming a Bat Mitzvah is very special. It is the day when a Jewish girl celebrates her entry into adulthood, usually shortly after she turns thirteen. It is an extremely important, wonderful celebration (Jewish boys have a Bar Mitzvah).

But becoming a Bat Mitzvah involves a *ton* of work. At least one year in advance you have to start taking lessons to prepare you for the Shabbat when you become a Bat Mitzvah. (Shabbat is the holy day of the week for Jewish people, from Friday at sundown to Saturday at sundown.) To become a Bat Mitzvah, you have to read a portion of the Torah, which is the first five books of the Bible written in Hebrew. The Torah contains stories, laws, and history of the Jewish people.

Hebrew. This is a language I am studying (not very well) to become a Bat Mitzvah. That is one of the reasons it takes so much work to become a Bat Mitzvah. I have to sing (yikes!) another part of the service, the Haftarah, a reading after the Torah.

So you read (actually you chant more than sing, in Hebrew). And then in my synagogue, you also have to give a speech (which the rabbi keeps calling a sermon, which makes me even more nervous). And then there is usually a party. All your relatives come and give you gifts and big hugs and kisses and tell embarrassing stories about when you were a little girl.

At least, that's what will happen at our Bat Mitzvah, if I know some of our relatives. And practically *all* of our relatives, it seems, were attending the big event. Mom, who once took classes at the Culinary Institute of America (she calls it the CIA — Anna and I used to tell other kids that our mother worked at the CIA), was planning a huge Friday night dinner to celebrate.

We had even sent out printed invitations — heavy, purple paper; thick, curly white lettering; the whole bit. *And* we were going to go shopping for special dresses to wear. Our Bat Mitzvah was going to be big. Huge. Wedding-sized, practically.

All that work, and all those details, can sneak up on you, no matter how fast you move. So as much as I was looking forward to it, I was also beginning to worry, *really* worry, about my part of the Bat Mitzvah.

For one thing, I wasn't keeping up with everything as well as Anna was. And for another, maybe, just maybe, I had let spring fever lead me into playing soccer and taking baby-sitting jobs when I should have been doing school work and practicing my Hebrew.

Anna, on the other hand, had managed to keep up with her two hours of violin practice every day, plus belong to the orchestra, plus do her schoolwork, *and* shine in Bat Mitzvah lessons.

We turned up the sidewalk to our synagogue.

Anna sighed.

I frowned. "Something wrong?"

"No," replied Anna. She sighed again.

"You're sighing. Something's wrong."

"Well . . ." Anna said. "I guess there is. I keep thinking about the speech."

The way she said it, I knew that both words were in capital letters in her mind: THE SPEECH.

Anna continued, "Every time I think about standing up in front of everybody, all our

7

friends and relatives, everyone at the Shabbat service, I feel, well, sick."

This truly amazed me. "Anna," I said, "You've played a solo with the high school orchestra on Long Island! You've stood up in front of judges and won violin competitions! How can making a speech scare you?"

"I don't know, but it does." Anna wrapped her arms around her violin case and hugged it to her chest, almost as if it were armor. "It's different when I play the violin. I forget where I am. I even forget who I am. I don't think about anything. I just play."

I considered that for a moment. Times like that occurred in sports, too. Suddenly running wasn't hard, it was easy. You floated above the ground. And then, just as suddenly, the race was over, or the game finished, and you looked up in surprise. At that moment, your feet came down on the ground again, hard.

I remembered, too, the dazed expression on my sister's face when she finished a performance and the audience began to applaud. She always looked a little startled. I realized now that it was because she had forgotten other people were even in the room with her.

She'd come down to earth, too. Hard. And it was only then she saw the audience.

"You'll do fine," I reassured her. "After you say the first few words, everything will fall into place, just like a violin piece. And you've got a good speech."

Actually, we'd worked on our speeches together. Anna was going to talk about some of the changes that we'd been through, and becoming a Bat Mitzvah. I was going to talk about the travels ahead and becoming an adult.

Anna nodded. But she didn't stop clutching her violin case as we walked through the doors into the synagogue.

CHAPTER 2

Rabbi Dorman was waiting for us. He seemed glad to see us and didn't seem to notice that we both, for separate reasons, looked less than happy to be there.

"Come on in," he said, waving us to the table on one side of his office.

The office, I decided, was a lot like Rabbi Dorman himself. It was friendly and interesting and full of unexpected surprises. The rabbi liked plants and both windows in his office were full of them. The light that came in filtered through a jungle of hanging spider plants and ivy, fat cacti, and jade plants. Some of the plants looked as if they were on their last leaf, but it wasn't because Rabbi Dorman didn't have a green thumb — it was because he couldn't help "rescuing" plants he saw dwindling away in grocery stores and shops.

Another thing I liked about the rabbi was

that the first thing he did, before he began our lessons, was give us this cool book to read called *Turning Thirteen*. It was about a girl who is afraid she'll lose her best friend unless they prepare for their Bat Mitzvahs together. The rabbi had used that book to talk about the reasons people have a Bar or Bat Mitzvah and what becoming a Bar or Bat Mitzvah means.

I'd never really thought about it before. In my mind, it was this big party that was somewhere in the future. Gifts were involved. *Lots* of gifts. That was about it.

Bat Mitzvah is Hebrew for "daughter of the commandment." When I became a daughter of the commandment, I would become a part of the adult Jewish community, not just my synagogue, but the whole Jewish community all over the world from Australia to Africa to Alaska.

"The celebration of becoming a Bar Mitzvah or a Bat Mitzvah is a tradition rooted in the commandment to study Torah," the rabbi was saying now. "Bar Mitzvah, the celebration for a Jewish boy coming of age, has been around since the Middle Ages, but Bat Mitzvahs have been celebrated only in this century."

I remembered when my Mom announced on our twelfth birthday that it was time to start preparing for our Bat Mitzvah. Then she showed us pictures of her own service and the next thing we knew, we were taking lessons with Rabbi Dorman.

"How is the Torah portion coming along?" Rabbi Dorman asked us.

"Great," said Anna.

I began to calculate how much more work I had to do.

Calculate. An unfortunate choice of words. Calculate was exactly what I wasn't doing well these days.

Although a great soccer practice had helped put it out of my mind, the memory of the math quiz I'd gotten back earlier in the day, with a big red "F" across the top, returned in full force.

My teacher said my mother had to sign it, to prove she'd seen it. *Honestly*, I thought indignantly. It's not as if I wasn't going to tell Mom about it. It's just that I wasn't going to tell her about it right away. I wanted to wait until the time was right.

Like when I was twenty-one.

"And you, Abby?" asked Rabbi Dorman.

"Huh? Oh. Great," I said.

Rabbi Dorman smiled. "You've still got time yet. Don't worry. Now, let's get to work."

We got to work. But I had trouble concentrating, even though we were studying the history of the Hebrew bible, which was very interesting. I had too much to think about.

"What *were* you thinking of?" demanded my mom.

Post-dinner test-signing time. Not the perfect time to ask my mom to sign off on a flunked math test, but I figured it was better than waking up at dawn when she was drinking her coffee alone in the kitchen.

"It wasn't totally my fault," I answered quickly. "I'd been out for two days before that, remember? With a cold." I pointed to the date at the top of the test.

"Did you tell your teacher? What's her name? Ms. Frost?"

"Yeah. But she said, 'tough,' and made me take it anyway." I tried to look righteously indignant and pathetically victimized.

My mother's brown eyes narrowed. "That's not right! Did you show her the note I wrote to your homeroom teacher?"

"Ms. Frost didn't care," I said. (She hadn't. That was true.)

"You tell Ms. Frost," said my mother, folding up the test and sticking it into her briefcase, "that I'll give her the signed test back tomorrow in person. I have a few things I'd like to say to her."

Uh-oh.

"Mom! That's okay. I mean, it's just one test. I'll make it up."

"Abby, I'm not about to let a teacher treat one of my daughters this way. In fact, I very much hope I wouldn't let a teacher treat any child this way. Injustice is injustice."

"But . . ."

Mom suddenly smiled. "I won't embarrass you, Abby, I promise."

What else could I say? I gulped, and nodded, and left.

I'd told my mother the truth — and I *didn't* think what Ms. Frost had done was fair. But I also knew that I'd spent most of the second day I was home from school watching reruns on TV, including a *Leave It to Beaver* marathon. After that, I'd studied the translation of the Haftarah, and finished reading a book on the Shabbat service that the rabbi had given us. I could have kept up with my math homework instead of watching Wally and the Beav. But I hadn't. I'd been counting on Ms. Frost's being sympathetic.

She hadn't been. And when I said that I was afraid that looking at all those numbers would cause me to have a severe relapse, she hadn't even cracked a smile.

"Abby. You haven't been giving math your full attention for some time now. I don't see that two days out with a cold makes that much difference," Ms. Frost had said, folding her arms.

I folded mine.

We looked at each other. I gave up and took the test and flunked.

So there was some nastiness on both sides in this situation.

Things went from not nice to worse the next afternoon. I spent the whole day dreading my mother's visit to school. The expression on Ms. Frost's face when I told her my mother was bringing the test in personally didn't help.

Ms. Frost knew she was being set up. And even though she deserved it, sort of, I felt bad.

The last bell rang and I leaped from my seat. Maybe my mom hadn't been able to get off early. Maybe her train had been delayed. Maybe she'd reconsidered and decided to mail the signed test back to my teacher.

I dashed into the hall and headed for my locker, vowing to do my math homework first that night, even before the Bat Mitzvah homework.

I stopped as I saw my mother push open the door of Ms. Frost's room and step inside.

Slowly I started forward again. I didn't mean to eavesdrop. I'm not sure what I meant to do. Somehow, though, I found myself standing outside the partially open door, listening to my mother talk to Ms. Frost.

"But Mrs. Stevenson," I heard Ms. Frost say.

"I'm not finished," snapped my mom. "I'd appreciate it if you would do me the courtesy of listening to what I have to say, a courtesy you apparently don't extend to your students."

Uh-oh!

"Now just a minute," I heard Ms. Frost say indignantly.

But my mother was on a roll. Keeping her voice firm and calm and steely cold, she cross-examined Ms. Frost like a prosecuting attorney on a television show. By the time my mother was finished, Ms. Frost had admitted that she had refused to give me extra time for the test, even though she knew I had been out sick. Ms. Frost didn't even have the chance to work in the information that I wasn't the best student and maybe hadn't earned any kind of special treatment — and that maybe, just maybe, I should have been able to do my math homework and stay caught up on my own.

Although she tried.

I heard a chair push back. "I trust this won't happen again," said my mother.

Ms. Frost said something indistinct and neutral.

"Good," said my mother. "Well, I've enjoyed talking to you."

I hadn't enjoyed the talk. Not one bit. I suspected Ms. Frost hadn't either. I knew that now, for sure, I was on Ms. Frost's bad side.

And that I hadn't been any more fair with her than she had been with me.

Great. Any way you looked at it, the situation added up to trouble. And there was nothing I could do about it.

CHAPTER 3

"This meeting of the Baby-sitters Club will now come to order."

With these immortal words, our fearless leader and BSC president Kristy Thomas kicked off the Wednesday afternoon meeting of the BSC at Claudia Kishi's.

All the regulars were there: Kristy; Claudia, the vice-president; Stacey McGill, our resident math whiz, and therefore the treasurer; Mary Anne, the secretary; me, the alternate officer; Mallory Pike and Jessica Ramsey, the junior officers. Absent were our associate members, Shannon Kilbourne and Logan Bruno. The associate members aren't required to attend regularly, since their main function is to take jobs when we have an overflow.

But all the rest of us have to be Present, and On Time.

On time is five-thirty every Monday, Wednesday, and Friday afternoon. We meet for half an hour in Claudia's bedroom, because she is the only BSC member with her own phone line. Our clients know they can reach up to nine experienced and very good baby-sitters by calling during those hours. And with Claud's line, we don't tie up anyone's family phone.

Every Monday, we hand over dues to Stacey. The dues are used to pay Kristy's brother Charlie for gasoline when he drives her and me to meetings (since we live so far away from Claudia's), for celebrations, and for supplies: from fliers, when needed to advertise the BSC, to the contents of the Kid-Kits. The Kid-Kits (a Kristy Idea) are boxes filled with inexpensive toys, games, books, puzzles, and so forth. Things we or our siblings have outgrown go into the kits, as well as new items, such as crayons and paper, from time to time. Jessi has a Kid-Kit with an office theme, including those funny little memo stick-ums that say things like "From the desk of the Boss." When we know we're going to be dealing with a child who is in bed with a cold, or a new client who might be difficult, or a houseful of kids and a sky full of bad weather, we take the kits along. They're always a big hit. The kids love having new toys to play with — even our old recycled ones.

We also write, every single meeting, in the

club notebook. (Another Kristy Idea). That's where we keep a record of who we sat for and what happened. We are all responsible for reading the notebook once a week, to keep ourselves up-to-date on what's happening with our regular clients, and what new clients are like.

Another club book is the record book, kept by Mary Anne (who's never, ever made a mistake!). It contains our client list, with names, addresses, and phone numbers, plus each member's schedule of extracurricular activities and baby-sitting jobs.

It all sounds very professional you say? But of course.

After all, we're a business. A very successful one, too. Even before I joined, the BSC hardly ever had to get new business by putting up fliers in supermarkets or handing them out to potential clients. Our satisfied customers are our best advertisements, and we got all the business we needed by word of mouth.

Whose brilliant idea was the club? Our fearless leader's, of course. One night Kristy was listening to her mother call one baby-sitter after another, trying to find a sitter for Kristy's little brother, David Michael. Suddenly Kristy realized how much more organized and efficient (the building-block words of Kristy's vocabulary) it would be if her mother could just dial one number and reach several experienced and reliable baby-sitters.

In no time at all Kristy had formed the Baby-sitters Club with her best friend, Mary Anne, who lived next door at the time, and their good friend Claudia Kishi, who lived across the street. Soon they had more business than they could handle. That's when Stacey joined. She'd just moved to Stoneybrook from New York City with her parents. Stacey and Claudia soon became best friends. And not long after that, Mary Anne met Dawn Schafer and she became Mary Anne's other best friend — and joined the BSC. Mallory Pike and Jessica Ramsey, who are both in sixth grade (Mallory used to be one of our baby-sitting charges), followed as junior officers. Because they are in sixth grade, they can't take nighttime sitting jobs, except with their own families. Logan and Shannon joined as associates, to cover jobs that we couldn't take ourselves.

Kristy is a small person (the shortest person in the eighth grade at SMS) with big ideas and bulldozer effectiveness. She Gets Things Done. Sometimes she is less than tactful. Some people even call her bossy. But I think that the people who call her bossy are mostly just not comfortable with a girl being so sure of herself.

Since I am outspoken and self-confident myself, and since Kristy and I don't always agree, it means we clash sometimes. But I admire Kristy's style. I think the world needs more Kristys.

When Kristy came up with the idea for the BSC, she was living in a small house packed to the roof, practically, with her family: her mother, her two older brothers, Sam and Charlie, and her younger brother, David Michael. Her father had walked out on her family when David Michael was just a baby, and things hadn't been easy.

Then Kristy's mother fell in love and got married — to a millionaire! They all moved to his house, which is a real, live mansion, where they have plenty of room.

Then their family became even bigger. Watson's two children from his previous marriage, Karen and Andrew, stay there a lot, of course. Plus Watson and Kristy's mom adopted a Vietnamese orphan, a baby they named Emily Michelle. After that, Kristy's maternal grandmother, whom everybody calls Nannie, came to live with the family to keep an eye on things and help out. Add to that a Bernese mountain dog puppy, a cranky cat, some goldfish, a hermit crab, and I-don't-know-what-other assorted pets *and* a resident ghost (at least, that's what seven-year-old Karen Brewer believes is living in a room on the third floor), and you can see why Kristy has to be organized and efficient.

Kristy's best friend, Mary Anne Spier, is also organized and efficient, and pretty short herself. Like Kristy, she has brown hair and is a casual dresser (although Kristy's standard uniform, jeans and a sweater or sweatshirt, wins the most-casual award hands down). And like Kristy, Mary Anne is part of a blended family. But they are also very, very different in many, *many* ways.

They grew up together on Bradford Court (where Claudia still lives), but while Kristy was surfing the churning waters of a big family, Mary Anne was an only child, and a half-orphan. Her mother died when Mary Anne was a baby, and her father, to make sure that he wouldn't be an overindulgent parent, went in the opposite direction and was very strict. He even made Mary Anne wear little girl clothes and pigtails long after she was ready to start checking out a new look. I don't mean red lipstick and talon fingernails — just no pigtails, for example, and getting to choose her own clothes, such as jeans instead of dresses.

Maybe her dad's overprotectiveness is part of the reason Mary Anne is so painfully shy and so sensitive, too. I've never seen this, but I understand that even commercials on television can make her cry. Amazing.

The other side of Mary Anne's sensitivity is that she is a very good listener, and more than any of the rest of the BSC members, she is able to pick up right away on what other people are feeling. This makes her a super friend, and an excellent baby-sitter.

Because of Mary Anne's responsibilities in the BSC, she was at last able to prove to her father that she could handle a little more responsibility for her own life. Her father began to relax. He even let Mary Anne adopt her first pet, a kitten named Tigger. I should also mention that Mr. Spier was (and is) cool about Mary Anne's boyfriend, Logan Bruno.

So I guess you could say both father and daughter started growing up and doing fine.

And that's not all that happened. When Dawn and her brother and mother moved to Stoneybrook, they were moving back to Mrs. Schafer's hometown from California, where Dawn's parents had just gotten a divorce. And Dawn and Mary Anne discovered that once upon a time in high school, Mrs. Schafer and Mr. Spier had been sweethearts.

Mary Anne and Dawn did a little cupid work and before you could say "Here Comes the Bride" Mrs. Schafer and Mr. Spier had gotten married and had moved into the Schafers' old farmhouse.

So now Mary Anne has a larger family, and a haunted house of her own, just like Kristy's (yes, some people believe that a secret passage that Dawn discovered in the old farmhouse is haunted). But then Dawn's younger brother, Jeff, decided to move back to California to live with his dad, and Dawn missed them so much that she moved back, too.

We all still stay in touch with Dawn, though. I've met her a few times, and I like her. She's very easygoing. For example, in California, she helped start a West Coast BSC, the We ♥ Kids Club. But it has only a few rules, and isn't nearly as organized as the BSC (see Kid-Kits and notebooks, plural, above).

Dawn is very different from Mary Anne, too. She is tall and thin and has long, pale, blonde hair, blue eyes, and two holes in each earlobe. She's a surfer, but she doesn't have an extreme tan. That's part of her healthy attitude. She doesn't eat red meat and hardly eats sugar (she calls it poison). She is not only well informed about how important it is to take care of the environment, she is *passionate* about it.

Claudia, who is the vice-prez, both because she is one of the charter members and because she has her own phone, thinks that *health* food is poison. At every meeting, she provides the club with a mostly not health-food selection of junk food, from Twinkies to Pop-Tarts to

Double Stuffed Oreos. As an athlete, I have no objection to this. You need your carbohydrates, right?

And most of the other BSC members don't either, except maybe Stacey, Claudia's best friend (you'll see why in a minute). Anyway, Claudia's position on health food may not be exactly fashionable, but Claudia herself is a knockout. She's an artist, and possibly an artistic genius. Her eye for color and design extends to what she wears. She puts together outfits that most people couldn't even think of, and ends up looking as if she stepped out of one of the most cutting-edge fashion shows in the world.

Like today, when the predominant look was jeans and pullovers and Nikes, Claudia was in leopard-print tights, black ankle boots with fuzzy yellow slouch socks, black bicycle shorts, a yellow leotard, and this teeny, tiny fuzzy sweater with cap sleeves that was black with big yellow buttons. Her earrings were leopards: on one side a leopard looked as if it was coming through her earlobe toward you. On the other side, you could only see the back of the leopard, disappearing into her earlobe, as if her earlobes were these weird leopard cat doors.

She'd crinkle-braided strands of her black

hair, and tied the crinkled parts at the top with knots of yellow ribbon.

Totally impressive. In fact, a work of art.

The only thing that Claudia can't make into art is schoolwork. It just doesn't interest her. She has trouble with rules: spelling rules, math rules, writing rules. I believe creative people live by different rules, and it isn't exactly fair to expect them to think the way non-creative people think. But what can Claudia do? Until she's a rich and famous artist and can hire accountants and bankers and secretaries, she's got to struggle through, which is exactly what she does. Her parents even check her homework every night.

Claudia mystifies them, I think. Especially since her older sister is a regular genius in things like math and science. It's only recently they've begun to appreciate how cool it is to have two such different and amazing kids.

But her parents will never understand Claud's love of Nancy Drew books. They think of Nancy Drew as the written equivalent of junk food, which is a mystery, Claudia says, that even Nancy Drew herself will never solve.

If Claudia is creatively stylish, Stacey is classically in style. Some people in the BSC feel that Stacey is the most sophisticated of the club. She is definitely elegant. She's tall and slender, with blonde hair and a sort of New York City way of always keeping an eye on things, watching her back, if you know what I mean.

Stacey, who is an only child, moved to Stoneybrook from big old NYC with her parents when her father was transferred for his job. Then her father was transferred back to New York. Soon after, when her parents got divorced, her father stayed in the city and Stacey and her mother moved back to Stoneybrook for good.

Although I am not New York City sophisticated, I do feel as if I understand at least something about Stacey that the others don't. Because like me, Stacey has health problems.

Mine are asthma and allergies. Stacey has diabetes. That means that her body can't handle sugar well and she could get very sick, even go into a coma, if she doesn't watch what she eats all the time. No chocolate or candy. No pigouts. And she has to give herself shots of insulin every day to regulate the sugar in her blood.

For that reason, Claudia's junk food hiding places, which are located all around her room, from hollow books to coat pockets, always produce healthy junk food, too. Along with Sugar Frosted Flakes and Twinkies and Double Stuffed Oreos, she'll hand out pretzels, Frookies (cookies sweetened with fruit juice instead of sugar), popcorn, and even apples and oranges.

These are things Claudia wouldn't have to hide from her parents. But she stashes them away with the rest of the junk food just the same.

Mallory, like Kristy, is from a large family. She has seven brothers and sisters, including triplet brothers. She is the oldest in her family, which means that she has plenty of baby-sitting experience. And like Kristy, she isn't easily rattled.

I think Mallory is pretty cute. Like all her brothers and sisters, she has brown hair, although hers is more reddish brown than any of theirs. And she has pale skin and big brown eyes. But to Mallory's eternal despair, she has glasses and braces. She's working on per-suading her parents to get her contact lenses. The braces, she realizes, are something she is going to have to wait out.

Mallory wants to be a children's book writer and illustrator some day. She's definitely the person whose Kid-Kit has the most and the coolest children's books.

Jessi, like Stacey and me, moved to Stoney-brook from somewhere else. Jessi lives with her parents, a younger sister, Becca, a younger brother, Squirt, and her aunt who helps keep things running smoothly, just as Nannie does for Kristy's family.

Like Kristy and Mary Anne, and Stacey and Claudia, Mal and Jessi have much in common with each other. They both love horses and reading, particularly horse stories and mysteries (but *not* horror stories). But Mal is not particularly athletic, while Jessi is planning on being a prima ballerina someday. Both are pursuing their goals already. Mal has won a prize for her fiction writing, and Jessi, who studies ballet in special classes after school, gets up every morning at 5:29 A.M., one minute before her alarm goes off, to practice ballet at the *barre* her family has set up for her in the basement.

Physically, they are very different, too. Today, Mal was in the jeans and sweater mode, a variation of what Kristy, Mary Anne, and I were wearing. The rust brown sweater Mal had on made her pale skin look creamy and brought out the red in her hair. She looked nice, but basic, if you know what I mean.

Jessi, who is taller than Mal, has black hair, brown skin, and dark brown eyes. She is slender where Mal is more sturdy-looking. Today she had her hair pulled back into a dancer's knot at the nape of her neck. She was wearing a loose rose-colored turtleneck, a jean skirt, tights, and pale pink warmup leggings with her flat shoes. Even though we were just at a club meeting, she was sitting very upright, looking poised and graceful. You could tell she was a dancer.

A diverse group, as one of our teachers might say.

A very cool group, is what I would say.

In between calls, we complained about homework, gossiped about school, discussed club business, and munched out on the goodies Claudia kept passing around.

Naturally, I talked about my Bat Mitzvah.

Claudia and Stacey wanted to know if I'd decided what I was going to wear yet.

Kristy rolled her eyes in disgust.

Mary Anne laughed. "You're going to have to dress up too, Kristy. You can't go to Abby's Bat Mitzvah party in jeans."

Kristy made a hideous face, only half-kidding.

"Listen," I said, "the clothes thing is the least of my worries. All of our relatives are showing up for this. People I haven't seen since I was a baby. Some of them are staying with us, but Mom's already reserved rooms at the Strathmoore Inn for people, too."

"Wow," Mary Anne breathed. "Like a wedding."

I nodded. Anna and I were hoping that our Long Island friends would be able to come too. But, if you can believe it, our good friend Morgan was having her Bat Mitzvah the same weekend.

"Plus, I have younger cousins who are coming too. So I was wondering if the BSC could help me out. I mean, Mom is going all out and cooking a huge Shabbat dinner on Friday night and then we're going to the synagogue for services. But the younger kids can't come. So . . ."

"This is a job for the BSC," declared Claudia with a grin. "I mean, you can't leave lots of kids of different ages to roam free. Or even to just watch television."

Mallory nodded. "Television wars," she said wisely.

"What?" Jessi wondered.

"Well, everyone is always fighting over the remote control in our house," explained Mallory. "The triplets are monster channel surfers. And my parents say it is driving them crazy, that everyone is spending too much time in front of the television set."

"That's amazing," said Jessi. "My parents have been complaining about Becca becoming a television head, too. I mean, every time any of her friends come over, that's all they seem to do."

Mary Anne was flipping open the pages of the record book to the day before the Bat Mitzvah. I noticed, with a mixture of appreciation and stage fright, that Mary Anne had already crossed off Saturday, the day of the Bat Mitzvah. No sitting jobs were going to be scheduled that day, so the BSC could turn out to see Anna and me become Bat Mitzvahs.

"Write me in for Friday night," volunteered Claudia.

"Me, too," Kristy piped up.

"And me, too," said Mary Anne. She looked up at me. "Will three sitters be enough?"

"Yes," I replied. "But what if all of you aren't needed? That means you'll have turned down other jobs, maybe."

"Don't worry," said Mary Anne, writing the names carefully.

The phone rang and we returned to work. I snagged a Twinkie and leaned back against the desk. I was overworked and overextended. But at least I had one part of the Bat Mitzvah covered.

CHAPTER 4

Two weeks and panic time.

You don't have to be a mathematician to count up the days until your Bat Mitzvah and know they are not enough. I'd been going to class with Rabbi Dorman. I'd been listening to my Torah and Haftarah portions over and over again on my Walkman, hoping all those Hebrew words would sink in.

And I'd been trying to keep up in school, especially in math class. I didn't want to earn Ms. Frost's wrath. In fact, I didn't even want to earn her attention. So even though I wasn't exactly listening in her class, I was doing a good imitation. Ms. Frost's attitude toward me since my mom's parent-teacher conference had been a little, well, frosty.

When I say I'd been trying to keep up, this doesn't mean I'd been totally booking it. I'd been doing the minimum to stay out of trouble. Frankly, math was low on my list of priorities.

Neither math nor the Bat Mitzvah was on my mind when Ms. Frost cleared her throat to signal she was about to make an important announcement. I was thinking about *Leave It to Beaver*. This, in my opinion, is one of the weirdest shows in the world, stranger than anything on *Star Trek*. The Cleavers, in all their starch and polish, are a mystery to me, one I was pondering as Ms. Frost began to speak.

Then I heard these horrible, horrible words: ". . . the test tomorrow. Don't forget it will be twenty-five percent of your grade, so study hard! And good luck."

My head snapped up.

Was Ms. Frost giving me the smug eyeball? I smiled as if I had everything under control.

And the bell rang.

Test? *What* test? Had these four evil letters, in this particular combination, been said aloud in class before? Recently?

Numbly I gathered up my books and stuffed them in my pack. The test *had* to have been announced before this. No one else seemed shocked or surprised. No one else was complaining.

Twenty-five percent of the grade. Did this

ever happen on Planet Cleaver? *What* was I going to do?

It didn't take Albert Einstein to figure out that I had to pass that test if I wanted to pass the course, especially since I had flunked the last test.

And if I flunked this test, how could I explain it to Mom?

Crunch time. The only thing I could do was totally cram from that moment until test time tomorrow.

But I'd been planning to work on preparing for my Bat Mitzvah. I *needed* to do that. I mean, I had already decided to skip soccer practice so I could do that, which shows you just how serious it was.

Stay calm, I told myself. Cool. Collected. It couldn't be that bad.

That was my mature, adult self talking. The panicked little kid shouted back, "Are you joking? You're doomed! Your life is over!"

I realized that I was standing by my locker with my math book in my hand and that the hall was empty. I hadn't even realized I'd reached my locker and opened the door.

The warning bell rang. I slammed my locker door shut and ran, barely making it to the next class on time. I ducked down in a seat in the back, pulled out my math book, and began to cram for my math test like a little kid in a total panic.

I studied through lunch. I studied during gym. The horrible realization dawned on me as I studied that even by cramming, the chances were very good that I wasn't going to make it. I'd fallen behind with the last test, and I'd never quite caught up. Numbers spun in my brain. They crashed against my skull. Theorems rose and sank. Sets and subsets ran wild.

Doomed. I was doomed.

At the end of the day, I found myself back at my locker, my forehead pressed against the smooth green metal. My fingers fumbled at the combination. I was already experiencing numbers burnout.

I let the math book slide from my other hand. It landed on the floor with a satisfying thud. I looked down at it and hated it. How could Stacey be so good at math? How could she contemplate life as a banker or an accountant? Ugh.

Thinking of Stacey, I remembered that we had a BSC meeting that afternoon. I'd have to call Kristy and cancel. Double-ugh.

I gave the math book a less than gentle nudge with my toe, and listened to the sound

MARTINEZ SCHOOL LIBRARY

37

of book against locker. I pulled my foot back again.

A voice beside me spoke. "I hate math, don't you?"

I looked up to see someone who had a locker in the same row as mine, much farther down the hall. At least, that's what I assumed. I mean, I'd seen him around there before. He was the kind of guy who looks familiar without really standing out: jeans, flannel shirt, brown hair, brown eyes.

"Math," I said, "is evil."

"I know what you mean." He shifted his backpack from one shoulder to the other and looked around. Then he lowered his voice. "And that test is going to be a killer. Ms. Frost really wants to ice her students, if you know what I mean."

"Do I ever," I said bitterly.

The guy grinned. "But I've got a little ice of my own. A genuine, guaranteed study guide."

"Study guide?" My ears pricked up at that.

"The mysteries of Ms. Frost's math class revealed. Test results in the passing range. Guaranteed."

"You wouldn't want, to, uh, lend it to me?" I asked. "Like let me make a copy?"

He shook his head. He seemed amused by my question. "Nope. But I have an extra copy I'll sell you."

My heart sank. I hadn't been baby-sitting all that much because I'd been studying for my Bat Mitzvah. My funds were low. "How much?" I asked, feeling hopeless.

"Three dollars," he replied.

My heart leaped back up. I had three dollars. Not much more than the price of photocopying the thing, unless it was some monster-sized wad of pages.

"I'll take it!" I said, and dug into my pocket and pulled out three bills, top speed.

The guy pulled three pages, stapled together, out of his pack and handed it over. "This is a special study guide," he cautioned. "Don't go telling people you have it. And don't give it away to anyone else, okay?"

"Of course. Fine. No problem," I practically babbled, running my eyes over the first page. Even in my math-deficient state, I could see that this study guide was just perfect. It had it all: questions, answers, explanations.

"Thank you, thank you," I gushed.

"No prob,"said the guy again, and eased off down the hall. I picked up my math book, jammed it into my pack, then carefully put the study guide on top. I had a chance. I might pass after all.

It wasn't until much later, nearly bedtime, that I wondered for a moment about the study guide. I mean, it was so excellent. I wasn't even going to have to pull an all-nighter. I might even feel like getting up early in the morning and studying my Bat Mitzvah lessons, maybe working on my speech.

Was it possible the guy was in my math class, and I'd never noticed him before? I didn't think so. So, then, he had to be in one of Ms. Frost's *other* eighth-grade math classes. I knew Mary Anne was in one.

But how had he known I was a student of Ms. Frost's? Because of the math book I'd dropped? But all the kids in the eighth grade had the same math book.

I looked down at the study guide. It was in math test format. I worked the problems and then checked the answers. With the correct answers available, I was able to figure out where I'd gone wrong when I didn't get the right answer.

Had that guy gone to the trouble of going through Ms. Frost's old tests? Did he have an older brother or sister who had had her?

I thought back to my school in Long Island. There had been a couple of teachers who taught the same thing the same way year after year. If you had an older sibling who'd had those teachers, you didn't even have to take notes — that is, if your older brother or sister had taken notes.

Was Ms. Frost like that? She didn't seem to be. I wasn't crazy about her, but she seemed to be a teacher who at least spent time trying to make her classes somewhat interesting.

Oh well. I worked a little longer, then pushed the chair back from my desk and yawned. I was going to get some sleep after all, and I wasn't going to have math nightmares. I wasn't going to ace the test. But I was pretty sure I wasn't going to flunk it, either.

I remembered something my mother had once said: it's not that women can't be carpenters or mechanics or anything else. Anybody can. You just have to be given the right tools for the job.

The right tools for the job. This study guide had definitely been the right tool.

Feeling pleased and maybe even a little smug, I went to bed.

CHAPTER 5

Monday

The parents have spoken. My seven siblings
are not happy.

I believe it, Mal. Even
when my father was
making me wear pigtails,
he never banned television.

Yeah. That's terible! Jerry Prezzziohso
thinks its a plott. That all the parnts got
togethar and said no to telavision.

It wasn't a plot of course, but it seemed that way on Monday afternoon when Mary Anne, Mal, and Claud began their after-school sitting jobs, the Monday I was cramming for my math test. It all started so innocently.

Mary Anne was looking forward to an afternoon with the Arnold twins, who live near her. Marilyn and Carolyn Arnold are both in second grade. They have brown hair, and wear silver rings on their right pinkies, and beaded ID bracelets on their left wrists. Apart from the ID bracelets, and different haircuts, the easiest way to tell them apart is to remember that they have an identical mirror image birthmark: Carolyn has a tiny mole under her left eye and Marilyn has a tiny mole under her right eye.

Marilyn, who is also slightly more outgoing, is musically talented, just like my sister Anna. Even though Marilyn is only in second grade, she practices her piano for at least half an hour every day, and she has taken lessons since she was four. Carolyn, on the other hand, is tone deaf (unlike me; I can hear music, I just can't carry a tune) and is always carrying around an official-looking notebook and a pen in order to write down her scientific observations of the world — sort of a Harriet the Spy of the natural sciences.

Mrs. Arnold, departing in a jingle of bracelets and a kaleidoscope of accessories for an appointment, said, "Mr. Arnold may get home before me, but if not, I'll be back in no more than two hours."

"Fine," replied the unsuspecting Mary Anne. Then she asked the routine question. "Any special instructions?"

She didn't expect any. Since the Arnold family has been a BSC client for a long time, we all know where the emergency numbers are posted and so forth.

Mrs. Arnold shook her head. She opened the door. "Well," she said casually. "Just one thing."

Mary Anne, who was looking around for the twins and feeling a little surprised that they weren't there to say hello, said, "Oh?"

"No television." Mrs. Arnold smiled as if this were nothing. "They're a little annoyed, of course, since Jack and I pulled the plug on it this past weekend, but they'll come around. I've told them, they have plenty of inner resources. They're bright girls and capable of entertaining themselves. Don't worry."

She waved and was gone.

Slightly shaken by this news, Mary Anne walked toward the den calling, "Carolyn! Marilyn! It's me! Mary Anne . . . "

Two unsmiling faces turned toward her.

Carolyn was stting on the sofa with her arms folded.

Marilyn was sitting in the chair across from her with *her* arms folded.

The television, a big silent black eye, was across from them.

"Hey!" said Mary Anne, pretending she didn't notice the sulks taking place.

They glared at her.

Then Marilyn unfolded her arms. She narrowed her eyes. "*Now* can we watch television?" she demanded.

Meanwhile the triplets were at the park playing baseball. Mal was grateful for that. She had her hands full with Vanessa, Nicky, Margo, and Claire.

She had been startled but not terribly upset when her parents had announced on Friday night that this weekend marked the end of the television era at the Pike house.

"We're canceling cable," her mother had said. "No television during the week. And the only television on the weekend is family style — something the whole family can watch together."

The triplets had gone into shock. Vanessa, Nicky, and Margo had protested vehemently. Only Claire, age five, hadn't seemed to be hit by the full import of the news.

Until that Monday afternoon when everyone got home to find that the cable had been cancelled. And that the plug had been removed from the television.

Mal watched in despair as Claire hurled herself to the floor in the classic temper tantrum pattern that the BSC had believed she was starting to outgrow.

She wasn't. She pounded her fists. She kicked her feet. Her face turned red. And she howled, "Nofe air! Nofe air!" over and over.

"Hey, it's a cool day outside. Why don't we go out and play?" suggested Mal.

Claire howled on.

Vanessa said scornfully, "Play? No way."

Nicky stuck out his lower lip. "I want to go to the park with Adam and Byron and Jordan."

Margo said, "The Mr. Pinhead show is on. I want to waaaatch!"

Mal knew it was going to be a long, long afternoon. She wondered if she could charge double time because of the unusual situation.

Andrea Prezzioso didn't know she couldn't watch television. She was a baby. Watching the mobile spin over her head was enough for her.

Jenny knew. Finicky Jenny Prezzioso got some of her best finicky ideas from watching television. She was, Claudia suspected, a future patron of the home shopping channels.

In fact, Claudia had been at the Prezziosos' more than once and found Jenny hanging on to the descriptions of strangely shaped lockets and oddly named perfumes that were being sold on television infomercials.

Jenny wasn't watching television now. She was watching Claudia.

Claudia repeated her statement. "Give me the remote, Jenny. And turn off the television. You know your parents have made a new rule."

"I don't care," declared Jenny.

"I do," countered Claudia. She held out her hand.

Jenny and Claudia stared at each other. Claudia really wanted to blink, but she knew if she did, she was dead.

Just when she thought Jenny was going to outlast her, Jenny drew her arm back and hurled the remote. Claudia ducked instinctively, but Jenny was just throwing it at the sofa cushion.

"Fine!" she shouted. "I don't care."

She stormed out of the room and Claudia heard Jenny's bedroom door slam.

The sound of the slam woke Andrea in her room. She began to cry.

Claudia sighed. She felt as if she were in a

bad horror movie, where all the kids' minds had been taken over by television.

"Coming, Andrea," she called. She picked up the remote and put it up high on the bookshelf before she left the room.

"We could go visit Elvira," suggested Mary Anne. Elvira is a baby goat that lives on the Stones' farm, not too far away. A nature walk to visit Elvira and the farm (which also includes chickens, cows, a goose named Screaming Yellow Honker, and often cookies or a snack with Mrs. Stone) is usually a fail-proof suggestion.

This time it failed.

Marilyn rolled her eyes and sighed. "We've *seen* the goat," she said in an aggrieved tone.

"Yeah," said Carolyn.

They rejected several other suggestions and Mary Anne finally did what every desperate baby-sitter has been known to do from time to time.

She resorted to bribery.

"Let's go visit Mrs. Towne," she said, referring to another neighbor who lives nearby. Mrs. Towne, a small, independent woman with soft, faintly wrinkled brown skin and short white hair, is also a favorite of the Arnold twins. Her gardens always have something interesting growing in them, and she is well-known for her needlework, particularly her quilting. Mary Anne has taken sewing lessons from Mrs. Towne and still likes to visit.

"And when we get back, we can have a special treat," Mary Anne hurried on, when she realized that visiting *anyone* was not going to interest the unhappy, television-deprived twins today.

"Something really good to eat?" asked Marilyn.

"Anything we want?" added Carolyn.

"Something really, really special," Mary Anne promised. She wasn't exactly saying that the twins could have any treat they wanted, but they seemed satisfied with her promise.

They set off to visit Mrs. Towne, not cheerfully, but at least without complaining.

Now all Mary Anne had to do was think of a really, really special treat.

As it turned out, Mrs. Towne was watching television and working on one of her patchwork quilts. But she turned off the set as she led Mary Anne and the twins onto the sunny, glassed-in porch where she'd been working.

"That's okay," said the twins together, something they often did and never seemed to notice.

"You can leave it on," said Carolyn, her eyes

suddenly glued to the small, now blank screen almost hidden by the jungle of plants growing on the porch.

Good grief, thought Mary Anne. They'd barely gone a day without television and they were acting as if they were being tortured.

"Heavens, no! It's just television," said Mrs. Towne, laughing. "You girls sit down and I'll go and see if that chocolate cake I baked this morning is ready to be tested."

"Chocolate cake!" That got Carolyn's and Marilyn's attention, so much so that they didn't protest.

"This is our special treat, isn't it?" asked Marilyn, smiling. "How did you know Mrs. Towne had chocolate cake?"

Mary Anne didn't bother to explain that she didn't know. She just sank back against the overstuffed cushions of the rattan chair in relief. The twins and Mary Anne spent the rest of the afternoon talking and eating chocolate cake and admiring Mrs. Towne's latest needlework. By the time they were ready to leave, Marilyn and Carolyn seemed to have forgotten their television blues. And if they were a little too full of chocolate cake to make the most out of dinner, Mary Anne wasn't going to let it bother her.

As far as she was concerned, Mrs. Towne and her chocolate cake had saved Mary Anne from a nightmare baby-sitting afternoon.

As they waved good-bye to Mrs. Towne, Mary Anne suddenly remembered the slogan she'd seen on a T-shirt. "When in doubt, eat chocolate."

Today, it had worked.

Mal didn't have any chocolate. She had four angry kids who weren't interested in any of the things they usually liked: dress-up, tag, baking, hide-and-seek. Claire stopped her temper tantrum only because everyone else ignored her. But she kept sniffling.

Finally Mal lost her temper. "You want to sit around and sulk?" she asked. "Fine!" She pointed at a chair. "Vanessa, sit there. Nicky, you sit over there. Margo, you sit there. Claire, you sit next to Margo."

Mal sounded so tough that every single one of them sat.

Mal sat, too. She folded her arms and scowled ferociously.

After three minutes, Claire sniffled and said in a small voice, "How long do we have to sit here?"

"Don't talk," Mal ordered.

Two more minutes passed. Nicky wriggled. Vanessa stared out the window. Margo slid down on the sofa.

Claire asked, "Why can't we talk?"

"You can't talk because all you do is complain about no television. You can't move because you don't want to do anything anyway. So I'm letting you do what you want to do: nothing." Mal looked fiercer than ever.

Claire leaned back, wide-eyed.

Another minute passed. And another. At last Vanessa sighed and said, "I guess we could go outside. And play seek and hide." (Vanessa wants to be a poet and she often talks in rhymes.)

"Or tag," said Nicky tentatively.

Mal kept her fierce face on. "Maybe," she said.

"Please?" asked Margo.

"Please?" echoed Claire.

"Well, okay," agreed Mal. "Put on your jackets."

Everyone went outside and played hide-and-seek. Then they played freeze tag. Then they came back inside and drank juice and ate popcorn.

When the triplets and Mal's father hit the door, Mal congratulated herself on a job well done. One television-free afternoon, no problem.

She congratulated herself a little too soon.

"How'd it go?" asked Mr. Pike, hanging his jacket up by the back door.

Claire's lip poked out. Her eyes filled

52

with tears. "It was awfulllll," she wailed. "Why can't we watch Mr. Pinheadddddd? Nofe air . . ."

"Jenny, come out of there," demanded Claudia. She jiggled the doorknob of Jenny's parents' room.

"No," said Jenny.

"Jennifer Prezzioso!" said Claudia more loudly, and then bit her lip. It had taken her a long time to get Andrea back to sleep. She lowered her voice. "Jenny!"

Jenny didn't answer. From the other side of the door, Claudia heard the sound of applause.

When Jenny had stormed out of the den, she hadn't gone to her room after all. She'd gone to her parents' room. The Prezziosos had a small television high on their bureau. Jenny had found the remote and had locked herself in her parents' bedroom to watch television.

"Jenny," said Claudia desperately, "your parents are going to be *very* upset when they find out what you did. But if you come out now, I won't tell them."

In answer, Jenny turned up the sound on the television. " . . . only nineteen ninety-five for this beautiful gold-luster necklace," Claudia heard.

"Jenny?" she said, giving the doorknob a final rattle.

Of course Jenny didn't answer.

Beaten by a four-year-old. Claudia couldn't believe it. She thought of shouting "Fire, fire!" but realized immediately that it was not the solution of a responsible baby-sitter. Was there a ladder in the garage? Should she try to climb up to the window?

She went outside to the garage. The only ladder was too short to reach a second floor window.

Claudia was stumped until she realized that she was staring at a neat row of tools hung against the back wall of the garage, including screwdrivers.

A few minutes later, Claudia was back outside Jenny's parents' bedroom door with an assortment of screwdrivers.

"Jenny, this is your last chance," Claudia warned her. "Come out now."

She wasn't sure, but she thought she heard Jenny giggle. The sound on the television became louder. Deafeningly loud.

With a sigh, Claudia knelt down and went to work on the doorknob.

The blare of the television masked the sound of Claudia loosening the doorknob and the hinges. But when she lifted the door up off the hinges, she lost control. It was a very heavy door and it slipped out of her hands to land in the Prezziosos' bedroom with a huge crash.

"Jenny!" gasped Claudia, struggling to keep her own balance and half falling into the room herself. "Are you all right?"

Jenny had dropped the remote and leaped back against the wall. Her eyes were huge.

Claudia straightened up and tried to appear calm and in charge. She picked up the remote and clicked off the television.

She heard the sound of a door opening, this time in the normal way. It was the front door.

"I'm home!" called Mr. Prezzioso. "Where are my girls?"

Jenny burst into tears.

CHAPTER 6

If anybody had asked me how I felt on Tuesday morning, I would have said smugly, "The numbers are in my favor."

While I knew I wasn't going to blow the math test out of the water, I also felt confident that I would pass, and pass easily. The study sheet had been solid gold. I resolved to find the guy who'd sold it to me and get my hands on some more study sheets as soon as possible.

Part of the smugness, too, I admit, came from the fact that I was going to do well on the test and I believed that Ms. Frost hoped I wouldn't.

I stretched and shook out my hands and feet as Ms. Frost handed out the test, just as I do before a big soccer game or track event. I gave Ms. Frost a big smile as she handed me the test.

She looked startled.

But not half as startled as I felt as I looked down at the problems on the page lying on the desk in front of me.

The first problem looked very familiar. Wow. It was the same as the first problem on the study guide. Had I lucked out, or what?

But then I realized that if I'd lucked out, it was bad luck. Because it wasn't just the first and second and third problems that were identical to the study guide I'd bought. It was *all* the problems. The test *was* the study guide. I'd bought a copy of the actual test.

Panic gripped me. I looked around wildly.

I glanced toward the front of the room.

Ms. Frost said, "Okay, class. You may begin now."

She sat down behind her desk.

I froze in mine. What was I going to do? I'd bought — stupid, *stupid* me — not a study guide but an actual copy of the test. Somehow that guy had managed to get his hands on it ahead of time.

My stomach lurched. I felt faintly sick. Could I convince Ms. Frost that I was too sick to take the test?

No, I didn't think so. And if I wasn't able to convince her, I'd have to take the test. Not taking it would mean a big, fat zero.

Okay, I reasoned. I would just answer the questions that weren't on the "study guide."

Fat chance. Every single question on the test had been on the study guide. I was trapped. I had to take the test.

The students around me had their heads bent, writing.

I bent my head, too. I took the test. I knew all the answers. And it gave me no joy.

I was the last person to hand my test in. I hoped that I'd get the courage to say something as I dropped the paper on Ms. Frost's desk as the bell rang.

But what could I say?

I laid my test on top of the other tests and walked out, without quite looking at Ms. Frost.

For the next three days, I stewed about that test. It hadn't been my fault, I told myself. I hadn't known I'd bought the *real* test. I'd never buy another.

But why didn't I just tell Ms. Frost that I'd made a mistake?

Because, after the way I'd set her up, I thought, she'd never believe me. How many people were dumb enough to believe they were buying a "study guide"?

Not only did the test haunt my waking hours, it haunted my dreams.

Only the dreams were all nightmares and I'd wake up with a gasp and discover I was sweating and tangled up in the blankets and had hurled the pillows off the bed.

The day after the test Anna asked, "Are you okay, Abby?"

"I'm fine."

"You sure?"

"Yes! Why are you picking on me?"

Anna looked surprised and a little hurt. "I'm not picking on you. You just looked — hassled."

I smiled a little at that. It was an old hippie word, one of the ones our father had used, sort of jokingly.

"I guess I am a little hassled," I admitted. I looked at my twin. Could I trust her? Could I pour out the whole horrible story and ask for her advice?

I took a deep breath. "I'm just worried about this Bat Mitzvah stuff. You know."

It wasn't a lie. It was part of the truth.

Anna nodded. "It's starting to worry me more and more. But you know what? That happens before performances, too. You sort of worry and worry and worry and just when you think you're going to go crazy, you get very calm. It's like, suddenly you've accepted your fate, or something. You know there's nothing you can do but just do it." She grinned at me. "Like that commercial you like. About the athletic shoes."

"I'll be glad when that moment comes," I said. But my mind was already spinning off into other directions. To become a Bat Mitzvah meant to become an adult, with an adult's responsibilities. Didn't that include telling the truth? Like about what had happened with the math test?

Maybe it wasn't even legal for me to become a Bat Mitzvah after something like this had happened.

We went into our separate bedrooms and I pulled out the book Rabbi Dorman had lent me. Each page had two columns, with the words of the Torah in Hebrew in the right column and the English translation in the left column. Hebrew is read from right to left, and you begin reading at what in most English books is the end.

Rabbi Dorman. For a moment, I considered talking to him. But I pushed the thought away.

And I studied my Torah portion.

With a guilty conscience.

CHAPTER 7

I didn't make a hundred on the math test. Not even by cheating.

I made a 98.

I took the test from Ms. Frost. She didn't say anything. I didn't either. I just stared at the big red numbers at the top. Then I looked at the answer I had missed. I knew it was the same answer as in the study guide. So the study guide had been wrong.

Such a good grade in any subject normally would have been cause for celebration. I would have slapped it down on the lunch table, mentioned it casually in conversation, and maybe even whipped it out to wave around at a BSC meeting.

But not this time. I folded the paper and stuck it in the back of my notebook and tried not to think about it. I'd passed the test. I was relieved it was over.

Maybe, in time, the guilt would go away.

I resolved that after my Bat Mitzvah, I would put myself on a regular study schedule and bring all my classes up to speed — especially math.

With any luck, and by avoiding all study guides now and forever, I should be able to stay out of trouble.

I kept my head down for the rest of the class, but I listened to Ms. Frost drone on about math. I took notes. I paid attention. Guilt was a great motivator.

Which somehow made me feel even guiltier.

I was glad when the bell rang and the class ended. In super fast forward, I gathered my stuff and jumped up.

Ms. Frost's voice stopped me. "Abigail. Could you wait a moment, please? I'd like to talk to you."

Her voice was cold. And for once, no pun is intended.

As I sat down again, Ms. Frost asked four other students to stay, too.

What was going on?

We exchanged glances.

"Take out the tests I just returned to you, please," said Ms. Frost. But the way she said it wasn't a request. It was an order.

We took out our tests.

"Now, I want all five of you to look at question number thirty-six."

We looked. On my test, it was the question I had missed. The one the study guide had missed.

The one, as it turned out, that all five of us had missed.

Uh-oh.

I looked around, puzzled. The other four students didn't look at all surprised. In fact, a couple of them seemed to be trying to hide smiles. What was going on?

Had they all bought the bogus study guides, too?

"This is *much* too big a coincidence," said Ms. Frost, her voice, if possible, even colder. "Can anyone explain to me how all five of you, students of unequal math strengths, made the exact same grade — the highest grades in the class — on this test, while missing the exact same question?"

More looks were exchanged among the other four students.

I frowned.

"Doesn't anyone have anything to say?"

One of the other students shrugged.

"Very well!" Two spots of angry color showed on Ms. Frost's cheeks. "Ve-ry well! Then I must assume the worst. I must assume that you all cheated. I have checked with Mr. Taylor, the principal, and we have agreed that you deserve to be punished. You are hereby suspended from school for three days, starting next Monday."

One of the girls gasped.

I sat like a stone. Suspended! Three days! I'd never been suspended in my life!

And how could it happen now, on the very week I was to become a Bat Mitzvah? Sudden anger surged through me. It wasn't fair. It wasn't right.

Seething, I raised my eyes from my test paper to glare at Ms. Frost.

But she had already turned to her desk. With her back to us she said, "You are dismissed. You may go."

I staggered out of the room in shock.

Behind me, as we left, I heard one girl say loudly to another, "Can you believe it? That witch!"

Rapidly, I put as much space between me and the other four students as I could. I had hardly ever spoken to any of them. I didn't know who they were. And I wasn't feeling particularly friendly at that moment.

Suspended.

The word drummed in my head. I walked through the rest of the day like a zombie. Forget turning over a new leaf. Forget paying attention in class.

I skipped lunch and went to the library and sat there, staring at the same page of my history book for the entire period. What was I going to do?

By the time the final bell rang, half-crazy with worry and all the voices saying, "You should've, you shouldn't have, you must, you should, don't, yes, stop, go," I practically sprinted for Ms. Frost's room.

She was sitting at her desk, going over homework papers. She looked up when I burst in. Her face gave nothing away.

"Abigail," she said in a neutral voice.

"I have something I have to talk to you about," I said.

"Go ahead," she said in that same neutral voice.

"I didn't cheat," I said. "Not on purpose I didn't. I didn't copy anybody's paper."

Ms. Frost didn't say anything.

I continued, "How could I? I don't even sit near any of those other people."

Another long pause. Then I said, "It was the study guide."

"Study guide?" Ms. Frost's voice sharpened. "What study guide?"

"The one this guy sold to me. The day before the test." Quickly I told Ms. Frost what had happened by my locker that past Monday afternoon.

When I was finished, Ms. Frost picked up a pencil and rolled it between her fingers.

Then she said, "I find this very hard to believe."

"But it's true!" I burst out. "Why would I lie?"

Ms. Frost said, "I find it very hard to believe that you would be so gullible about this so-called study guide. Surely you must have known — "

"But I didn't! How could I?" I cried.

"Who sold you this study guide?" asked Ms. Frost.

"I don't know," I answered. Seeing Ms. Frost's disbelieving look, I said angrily, "I'm new. I haven't been at SMS that long. I don't know that many people. And I don't know who this guy is."

"Don't know. Or won't say?"

That stopped me. It was true, I didn't know. But it was also true that I didn't want to rat someone else out.

"I don't know," I repeated at last.

Ms. Frost shook her head. "Not acceptable. The suspension still stands. Think about it, Abigail. Why are you protecting someone if you didn't know you'd bought a cheat sheet from him?"

At the word "cheat" I felt my own cheeks redden.

"Fine," I practically snarled. "Believe what you want."

"And I'm going to have Mr. Taylor call your house right now," Ms. Frost added, angry herself. "To inform your parents."

"Be my guest!" I stomped out of the room.

I stomped down the hall and got my books. I stomped out of the school.

When I reached the phone booth on the corner, I dropped change in and dialed our house. Mom was at work and Anna was at band, as I knew they would be. The answering machine was on. Using the remote code, I listened to Mr. Taylor's message. Then I erased it.

With luck, and if I played my cards right, my mother would never know I'd been suspended.

CHAPTER 8

Monday

The sky was blue.
The birds were singing.
Not an April shower
in sight. Or a
television show.
Which meant that
in spite of the
perfect weather, I
met plenty of
storm clouds when
I went to sit
for Matt and Haley
Braddock after
school.

Jessi knows the Braddocks well and had a regular sitting job with them for awhile not long after they moved to Stoneybrook. They are energetic and upbeat, and all the BSC members like baby-sitting for them. Both seven-year-old Matt (who is profoundly deaf and communicates in American Sign Language) and nine-year-old Haley (who can talk as fast in sign language as she can speak) are athletic and competitive. Matt plays for the little kids' softball team Kristy coaches, the Krushers, and they are normally ready for any adventure.

Until the no-television rule broke out among the parents.

Prepared by what had happened with Claudia, Mary Anne, and Mallory the previous week, Jessi wasn't too surprised when Mrs. Braddock told her that there were snacks in the kitchen, the phone number where she could be reached was by the phone, and that the children weren't allowed to watch television. (The Braddocks have a special cable box that prints what people are saying on the screen).

Jessi said, "Okay."

"Haley and Matt are in the basement," said Mrs. Braddock. "The television ban has been in effect for more than a week now, so they're over the initial shock. But they are still not taking it well. Good luck."

"Thanks," said Jessi glumly to Mrs. Braddock's departing back.

Sure enough, Matt and Haley were in the basement.

"Hi," said Jessi, signing and speaking.

Matt looked up. He signed hello. Unenthusiastically. Jessi could see that he and Haley were playing cards.

Also unenthusiastically.

"It's a beautiful day out," said Jessi. "Why don't we go outside?"

Matt shrugged. Haley shrugged.

Then Haley said, "Do you get to watch television at home?"

"When I want to. But I don't watch that much television. There's too much else to do," said Jessi. She was telling the truth.

But Haley scowled and asked, "Did Mom tell you to say that?"

"No!" exclaimed Jessi. She was indignant.

"We can't watch television at Vanessa's either," Haley told Jessi, referring to Vanessa Pike. "But if we went to visit Becca, we could."

"Becca's not home this afternoon," said Jessi firmly. She didn't mention that Becca had suddenly begun to watch a lot less TV ever since she'd heard about the ban.

"Oh," said Haley.

She looked down at the cards. Then she and Matt had a rapid conversation, only some of which Jessi could follow. Matt shook his head. Haley signed some more. Finally Matt signed, "Okay" and got up.

"We'll go outside," said Haley, as if she and Matt were doing Jessi a big favor.

"Gee, thanks," said Jessi, but the sarcasm was wasted.

They went out to the front yard. Matt signed, "Play pitch."

"Why not?" said Haley. Matt dashed back into the house to get the gloves and baseball.

Haley remarked, "Life without television is stupid."

"Ummm," said Jessi.

"'I mean, what are we supposed to do?"

This, Jessi recognized, was a rhetorical question, which meant that Haley didn't want an answer. Jessi was right. Haley stormed on, "So what if we watch a lot of television? Everybody does!"

Not anymore, thought Jessi, remembering the Pikes and the Prezziosos and the Arnolds. And Becca.

As if on cue, Claudia, who lived nearby, walked down the street with Mal. They had the entire Pike family (except for Mr. and Mrs. Pike) in tow.

"Wow," said Haley.

Just then Matt came out of the house and saw the crowd coming toward them. He began to wave wildly.

A few moments later the entire group had merged. And they were all complaining about the television rule.

About two minutes after that, Shannon, Kristy, her little brother, David Michael, her stepsister, Karen, her stepbrother, Andrew, and Linny and Hannie Papadakis appeared. Kristy's older brother Charlie had dropped the kids off to play in the neighborhood. Kristy and Shannon had volunteered to baby-sit.

"Good grief!" said Claudia.

Karen, her blue eyes wide behind her glasses, leaped into the middle the crowd. "Television has been banned forever at our house!" she exclaimed dramatically.

"Not exactly," said Kristy dryly. She came over to sit down beside Claud, Mal, and Jessi.

Hannie said mournfully, "We can only watch two hours a week. The whole week! Weekends included."

Vanessa clasped her hands and looked up at the sky. "I've missed *two* episodes of *Cassandra Clue's Casebook*. And I *know* she was about to solve the mystery of the missing diamonds."

Mallory commented, "You can tell Vanessa's really upset. She's not talking in rhyme."

Everyone sort of snickered.

Hannie said, "I could use some of my two hours and watch and tell you what's happening . . . but then we might have to give up *The Simpsons.*"

"I bet I know what happened in *Cassandra Clue's Casebook*," said Karen.

"What!" shrieked Vanessa.

"She was at the mine, right? And someone was sneaking up behind her?"

"Right," said Vanessa.

"They pushed her in!" Karen made a pushing motion with her hands.

"No way," said Nicky. "That'd be the end of Cassandra Clue."

"Not if she fell on a ledge," argued Linny Papadakis.

The five baby-sitters leaned back and let the kids argue. At least it was working off some of their energy.

Suddenly, Haley signed something to Matt, who perked up and signed back excitedly. Haley jumped off the steps and crouched down. She backed under the steps and peered out. "I'm Cassandra Clue," she intoned. "Trapped in the mine."

Matt rushed forward and gave her a push.

Haley let out a truly awesome scream. Everyone jumped and crowded forward.

"Oh, no!" cried Karen. "They've pushed

Cassandra down the mine!" She grabbed Vanessa by the arm. "What are we going to do, Marvella?"

Vanessa played along. "Oh, what will we do? Boo hoo for Cassandra Clue!"

Matt rubbed his hands together like an evil villain in an old movie. Byron sprang forward and clapped Matt on the shoulder. "Well done, Dangerous Dan. You'll get a big reward for getting rid of that pesky Cassandra Clue!"

Claire and Margo sat down by the baby-sitters and leaned forward, their eyes wide. Andrew soon joined them.

Before you could say, "Mystery, mystery, who can solve the mystery?" the formerly disgruntled, television-deprived kids had started acting out their own mystery series. And they kept going until the baby-sitters practically had to drag them home.

"Don't forget!" shouted Karen as the actors and the audience disappeared into the dusk. "Tune in next week, same time, same place, for the *True Adventures of Cassandra Clue!*"

CHAPTER 9

"I'll do it. But I don't like it," said Anna.

"You don't have to *do* anything," I argued. "You just have to *not* do one little thing. Don't say anything to Mom about me being suspended. That's all."

"I won't say anything. But you should tell her. Because if you don't and she finds out, it's going to be even worse."

"Don't worry. It won't happen," I said with more confidence than I felt. (I had taken the suspension notice signed by Ms. Frost and Mr. Taylor out of the mailbox last Friday.)

Anna shook her head.

She was still shaking her head when we got off the bus in front of Stoneybrook Middle School on Monday morning.

"Good luck," she told me. She gave me what was meant to be a reassuring pat on the shoulder. But I could tell she was worried. I gave her my best "no problem" smile.

"See you after school," I said.

Still looking worried, Anna turned and went up the steps into the school. As she disappeared through the front door, I saw her fumble in her pocket, then hitch her earphones into place. I knew what she was listening to: her Torah portion.

I patted my own pocket to make sure that my Walkman was inside it. I had some Torah studying to do, too.

But first I had to make it safely into the public library downtown. I turned and started walking casually away from the school.

Then I thought, stop acting so guilty. You're not *supposed* to be in school. You've been suspended, remember?

Suspended.

I'd persuaded Anna not to tell anyone — especially our mother. I told Anna to tell everybody in the BSC that Mom had let me stay home from school to work on my Torah portion. I hadn't told anybody but Anna the sordid details, of course. My fellow BSC members are all good friends, but I'm not that tight with any of them. I didn't want them to know.

I just had to make it through three days, and Mom would never find out.

There was one other small problem: Mom was at home all week. She'd taken the week off to get ready for the big Bat Mitzvah weekend and the onslaught of friends and relatives who were going to start arriving on Friday. When we'd come down to breakfast that morning, Anna and I had found Mom elbow deep in cookbooks at the kitchen table. She was still there when we'd left. She just reached the muttering and making notes stage.

Anna and I knew she was about to do some amazing cooking. It would be a feast. A celebration.

Too bad I didn't feel like feasting or celebrating. Too bad I was practically a criminal, an outcast.

Too bad I probably didn't deserve to become a Bat Mitzvah. . . .

Stop that, I told myself.

I'd reached the library. I pushed open the door and scoped the area for Claudia Kishi's mother, who is head librarian at the Stoneybrook Public Library. The coast was clear. I walked in, pretending I was a college student, and headed for the back corner of the library. I found a chair and a desk and turned the chair so I had my back to any passersby, like nosy adults or librarians.

I unloaded my backpack. I took out my Torah study book, plugged in my headphones, and began to go over my Haftarah.

Time passed. I began to get sleepy.

I switched off the recording and decided to

work on my speech for awhile. Anna had hers almost ready. Mine consisted of a bunch of lines, most of them crossed out or so badly written over that you couldn't read them anyway.

My speech was about the future. Becoming, in the eyes of the members of the synagogue and the members of our family, an adult.

I sighed. Right at that moment, the future looked pretty grim.

I looked at my watch. Practically lunchtime. At school everyone would be headed for the same table in the lunchroom. Kristy would be making gross cafeteria jokes. Mary Anne would be turning green. Claudia would be laughing. I wondered what Claudia was wearing today. I wondered if Stacey . . .

Puh-lease! I stopped myself. It sounded almost as if I were missing school. Even worse, it sounded as if I were missing the school lunches!

Hunger. That was it. I reloaded my pack and headed back downstairs.

The main floor of the library had filled up. College students were wandering around with armfuls of books. Older people were reading newspapers and magazines at the long tables. I thought I caught a glimpse of Mrs. Kishi in the children's reading room and I ducked out the front door in a hurry.

Because Mom was camped out in the kitchen this week, I hadn't even been able to make a sandwich to bring with me to the library, something that would have been less risky than venturing out.

Oh well. I smiled. I guess I could suffer through one fast food feast.

By the end of the day, I was burnt out on the library. I'd Torahed, I'd mitzvahed, I'd struggled unsuccessfully with my speech, and more successfully with my homework. One thing about being on suspension — I wasn't going to fall behind in any of my classes, particularly math. (I was going to call some classmates to get the homework assignments while I was out.)

Anna had orchestra that afternoon, but I didn't have anything to do until the BSC meeting. I headed home to dump my books, relieved that the first day of suspension was over.

Mom wasn't there. But sacks of groceries were lined up along one cabinet and a note on the refrigerator told me that she'd gone back out to do some more shopping.

I retired to the safety of my bedroom and stayed there until it was time for our BSC meeting.

"How's it going?" asked Mary Anne. She gave me a funny look. She must have thought it was so wild that my Mom was letting me stay home from school.

I snapped my fingers. "Like that," I replied, then changed the subject to baby-sitting.

Since I couldn't go to soccer practice the next afternoon, I took a baby-sitting job at the Rodowskys', a safe distance from my neighborhood. They hadn't been caught by the dread television ban as far as any of us knew, but I figured it would be easy to get Shea, Jackie, and Archie outside to play some soccer.

I congratulated myself on my foresight and planning. I didn't allow myself to think about being devious and sneaky.

The next day I went back to the library. Included in my planning and foresight was a predawn dash to the kitchen, to pack myself a lunch. I'd also made sure to eat a big breakfast. This was not hard because, since Mom was home and on a cooking roll, she met us with fresh juice, pancakes, and all the trimmings as we stumbled into the kitchen. The groceries were bursting out of the cabinets and the refrigerator was crammed. But the stack of cookbooks had been reduced to about half a dozen, plus several official-looking lists with things checked and circled and starred in different colors.

Very organized, our mother.

My Haftarah portion was going along great. My speech was still dead in the water. Sitting in the library all day was making me very restless and I stood up several times to flip through books with odd titles and to stretch. No one came to the section of stacks where I was hiding out, but I had a close call in the bathroom downstairs when I was pushing the stall door open. Mrs. Kishi entered.

I ducked back inside and considered sitting down and pulling my feet up so she couldn't see any part of me. Then I realized I was being truly paranoid. Mrs. Kishi wasn't going to recognize me by my shoes and socks. She wasn't going to start beating on the door and shouting, "Fugitive from school! Abigail Stevenson, come out with your hands up!"

Still, my heart pounded hard until Mrs. Kishi left. And I waited a long time after that just to be safe.

That afternoon Shea, Jackie, and Archie Rodowsky were instantly ready to go outside and play soccer — or any sport, for that matter. Their dog, Bo, was also more than ready to join in, slamming the soccer ball with his nose and yelping hysterically. Jackie is seven and known, with affection, among the members of the BSC as the "Walking Disaster."

But we didn't have any disasters this time, unless you count Shea kicking the ball into

Bo's old doghouse (which, as far as I can tell,
Bo never uses since he stays in the humans'
house most of the time) and Bo and Jackie
going in after it at the same time.

I closed my eyes as Bo went in headfirst,
barking happily, and Jackie slid in feet first.
Would the splinters in the doghouse pierce
the ripped jeans Jackie was wearing? Had
Jackie had his tetanus shots? Would we have
to go to the emergency room?

As I opened my eyes and ran forward, the
whole doghouse rocked, then tipped over in
slow motion, onto its back, so the door was
facing straight up.

"Cool," said Shea. Archie laughed.

Just as I got there, Bo's head and then Jackie's popped up through the open door. Jackie
was laughing and so, I think, was Bo.

"Cool," said Jackie, echoing his older
brother. He looked up at me. "That counts as
a goal, right?" he added.

We gave him the goal.

Jackie has the makings of an excellent soccer
player.

For a little while, I forgot all my troubles.

And when I got home that night, my soccer
gear in my bag and my cleats slung over my
shoulder, I was able to answer truthfully, more
or less, when Mom absently asked how my
day was.

"Soccer was fun," I replied. I managed to ignore the sharp look that Anna gave me.

Two days down and one to go, I thought the next morning as Anna headed into school and I turned in the direction of the library.

I'd survived. I'd made it. Plus I was all caught up on my homework and everything else, except my Bat Mitzvah speech. Not including all the sneakiness and deception I'd been employing, one could almost argue that I'd taken my unjust suspension and made something positive out of it.

This called for a celebration. And much as I liked the library, another day there was *not* my idea of celebrating. I shoved my hand in my pocket. I had the money from baby-sitting the day before, plus some.

Impulsively I turned in the direction of Stoneybrook's shopping area. I spent the rest of the morning ducking in and out of stores. None of the merchants seemed to notice that I was not in school, or maybe they didn't care.

In the early afternoon, I found myself outside Pizza Express. We had pizza delivered from the Express a lot, but I'd hardly ever actually eaten pizza in a restaurant. Why not? I thought, and pushed the door open.

I'd just settled down in a booth by the window with a deluxe slice of cheeseless veggie pizza and a large Coke when I saw a face peering through the window that made me lose my appetite.

I froze, pizza halfway to my lips, as if by not moving, I might become invisible.

My mother wasn't fooled for a moment. Her face disappeared from the window and I watched with a sinking heart as she marched to the door of the Express, jerked it open, and marched in.

She slid into the booth across from me and folded her hands on the table in front of her so tightly that her knuckles were white.

"How's the pizza?" she said.

I gulped. I more or less dropped the pizza on the plate. "Uh, hi, Mom."

We stared at each other. Finally I said, "So. I guess you're wondering why I'm here."

"Yes."

I considered lying. I considered saying I was skipping school.

I realized that only the truth would save me now.

I told the truth. The whole truth. Including where I'd spent the last two days.

"I see," said Mom when I'd finished.

That was the last thing she said. We drove home in silence. I couldn't think of anything else to say. Part of me wanted to beg. The other part of me felt that keeping quiet might give me a better chance of survival.

I went to my room and lay down on the bed. The long, quiet afternoon crawled by, punctuated only by the sounds of my mother in the kitchen.

Finally, right before Anna was due home, I heard my mother's footsteps in the hall. She knocked on the door and waited until I said come in. I sat up as she walked into the room.

"What you did," she said, "was wrong. You lied. You deceived me. You persuaded other people to lie for you."

"I never said anyone else — "

Mom held up her hand. "I'm not asking what Anna knew or didn't know, or for that matter what your friends knew or didn't know. I'm just saying that your actions have had far reaching — and negative — effects for everyone involved. I've always thought of you as honest. I am more disappointed in you than I can say."

I felt the sudden sting of tears behind my eyelids. I blinked them back with an effort. "I'm sorry," I whispered miserably.

Mom said, "Starting next Monday, you are grounded for one month. You may baby-sit. You may engage in your afterschool activities. However, that is it. No sleepovers. No visits from friends. No phone privileges. No parties."

I nodded. In spite of myself, I sniffled.

Mom is not any more demonstrative than I am. She reached out and took a tissue from the box on my dresser and handed it to me. As I took it, she patted my shoulder, just the way Anna had on Monday morning.

It made me want to cry even more.

"Abby," said Mom. "I do believe you about the study guide. I want you to know that. I know that you could never deliberately cheat. Ms. Frost had no business not giving you the benefit of the doubt. I suspect that she has let her own personal prejudices against you — and against your outspoken mother — interfere with her judgment."

"Thanks," I said, feeling slightly better.

"Tomorrow, after school," Mom continued, "I'm going to pay Ms. Frost another visit. And we're going to have a talk about this whole business."

"You don't have to do that," I croaked.

Mom had turned to leave. She looked back over her shoulder. "Yes, I do," she said, and was gone.

CHAPTER 10

I returned to school the next day feeling relieved, tired, sad, and apprehensive. Anna was sympathetically silent on the bus ride to school. I'd told Anna everything that had happened the night before. She knew as well as I did that nothing anyone could say or do would make things better.

But I couldn't even be comforted by the thought that at least they couldn't get any worse. I knew Mom would be there that afternoon to talk to Ms. Frost. That could very well make things worse.

I wasn't sure how. I wasn't sure what else Ms. Frost could do to me, or how much less she could think of me.

I decided to believe that I didn't care. I didn't care so much that it was all I could think of all day long. The minutes crawled by like years, and by the time we'd reached the last class of the day, I was trudging through the halls feeling as if I were a thousand years old. My head ached. My feet felt like lead. My books weighed a ton.

I was so out of it that I barely realized that Mary Anne was walking ahead of me. She was talking to someone whose back was turned to me, but who looked familiar.

"Mary A — " I began, then let my voice trail off. I recognized that plaid flannel shirt. And when the boy half turned to lift his backpack off his shoulder and reach inside, I froze.

It was him. The guy who had sold me the study guide. As I watched, I saw him hand a couple of sheets of paper to Mary Anne in exchange for three one-dollar bills. Mary Anne smiled up at him — good, nice, polite Mary Anne — and said thank you.

Then, as the boy walked away, she looked down at the piece of paper.

"Don't do that!" I shouted, racing forward. I dashed to her and grabbed the cheat sheet.

"W-what? Abby, what are you doing? What's going on?" Mary Anne looked totally shocked.

"That guy who sold you this. What did he tell you it was?"

"Brad Simon? He said it was a study guide for Ms. Frost's class. She's giving us a test the day after tomorrow and — "

"It's *not* a study guide," I said. I unwadded

the test, which was clutched in my fist, long enough to see that the format was the same as the study guide I'd bought. Some of the problems were the same, too, although not all of them. "It's a cheat sheet," I explained. Suddenly the truth came tumbling out. "I bought a study guide from that guy, too. So did four other students, kids who actually knew it was a cheat sheet — the test with the answers. I don't know how this kid is getting his hands on the tests ahead of time, but he is. And he's selling them."

Mary Anne's eyes were wide. "But how . . . ?"

"One of the answers was wrong on the cheat sheet. All five of us made the same grade and missed the same answer. We all got suspended for it. That's where I've been. Not studying for my Bat Mitzvah — *suspended*."

"Oh, Abby. Oh, how awful for you," said Mary Anne.

That's Mary Anne all over. I would have gotten a little choked up over her concern for me, but we had a crisis on our hands. It was almost time for our last class of the day, and there we were standing in the hall, holding a hot study guide in our hands.

Finally we agreed to meet after the last class and go straight to Ms. Frost's room. Mary Anne would keep the study guide, folded up, and not look at it. We would show it to Ms. Frost and tell her what had happened — and name names.

And that's what we did. After the longest last class in the history of the world, Mary Anne and I met and went to Ms. Frost's classroom. We ran all the way there, to make sure we would beat my mom. When we arrived, we were gasping for breath.

"We have to talk to you," I said.

"Urgent. It's urgent. Very, very urgent," added Mary Anne.

Ms. Frost said, "Very well."

Mary Anne produced the folded study sheet from her pack and laid it on the desk in front of Ms. Frost. "I just bought this from Brad Simon," said Mary Anne. "He told me it was a study guide. Abby saw me buying it and rushed to warn me that it wasn't a study guide, it was a cheat sheet for your test. She told me he told her he was selling her a study guide last week and she believed him and got suspended."

I have to say, I was amazed at Mary Anne, who is usually shy. Although her voice was soft, there was nothing shy about her words, or the firmness of her tone.

"Uh, I didn't know who he was until Mary Anne said his name," I added. "Now I do."

Mary Anne said, "I haven't looked at the study guide."

"I have," I said. "It's the exact same format as the study guide Brad sold me. Some of the questions are even the same."

Slowly, Ms. Frost unfolded the study guide. She ran her eyes down the first page, and then the second. She put the papers back on her desk and looked from Mary Anne to me.

She doesn't believe us, I thought. She thinks Mary Anne is lying. Sudden indignation flooded me. Who did Ms. Frost think she was, not to trust Mary Anne? Okay, so I was new at SMS. Maybe that gave Ms. Frost a reason to doubt me. But how could anyone who had known Mary Anne for any length of time at all think she would lie? Or cheat?

"It's the truth!" I cried. Loudly. Very loudly. "Mary Anne would *never* lie!"

Mary Anne jumped.

Ms. Frost looked startled.

Then Ms. Frost startled *me*. "I believe you," she said. "You know, you're the only one of the five students, Abby, who's come forward. I should have listened to you, I admit it. Taking that test was a mistake, but I don't think you deliberately, knowingly bought a cheat sheet. Especially not in light of this new evidence. You did the right thing, Abby. And so did you, Mary Anne. I'm proud of you both."

Whoa. Ms. Frost had taken the chill off. For the first time in what seemed like forever, I felt better. Lighter. The lead was gone from my feet, the burden lifted.

"Thanks," I said.

Mary Anne, of course, started to blush.

"Guess you're going to rewrite that test, huh?" I said.

"I am," said Ms. Frost. "I'm not sure how Brad is getting his hands on these tests, but I have a good idea it involves his student job in the principal's office, where the copy machine is. Don't worry, I'll take care of Brad. And the test."

"You'd better start studying, then," I told Mary Anne.

"And you, too, Abby," said Ms. Frost. "I think you should have a chance to take the test over. You can do it after school next week. I believe I can trust you and Mary Anne not to discuss the contents."

"You sure can," I said fervently. And, I thought wryly, remembering that I was grounded, I'd have plenty of time to study.

And that was the scene my mom walked in on. She marched in, prepared for battle. But when Ms. Frost started praising Mary Anne and me, the battle turned into an embarrassing brag fest. Soon I was blushing almost as much as Mary Anne.

At last I grabbed Mom by the arm. "I have to get home, Mom," I said urgently. "I have a speech to write."

And I did, too. Suddenly, I had a lot to say about the responsibilities of adulthood.

CHAPTER 11

Friday

Suddenly I feel as if I am in the middle of a children's soap opera. The Young and the Reckless. Another, Smaller World. The Ultimate Channel Surfing Adventure. In Real Life. Forget television...

By the next Friday of the great television ban, our suffering clients didn't seem to be suffering any longer. In fact, when Stacey arrived at the Arnolds' just after dinner carrying a Kid-Kit in case they were sitting mutinously in front of the blank television, she found them waiting, packs on their backs.

Mrs. Arnold said, "They have big plans for the evening, Stacey, I warn you. But I'll let them tell you. I'll see you after the show."

Their mother had barely gotten out the door before the twins hurled themselves at Stacey.

"What show?" asked Stacey.

"It's time to go," said Carolyn.

"I'm the theme song," said Marilyn. "They can't start without me."

"What?" said Stacey. "Slow down. What are you talking about?"

"Our show. *Boo Hoo, Cassandra Clue!*" explained Marilyn. With Marilyn holding onto one arm and Carolyn holding onto the other, Stacey found herself being dragged out the door.

"I thought it was called *Cassandra Clue's Casebook*," Stacey began.

Carolyn interrupted her. "No, no, *no*. That's television," she told Stacey scornfully. "This is our show. In the Pikes' backyard."

Stacey and the twins arrived in the Pikes'

yard to find a swarm of kids. A curtain made of old sheets was strung across the clothesline that was extended from the side of the garage. A haphazard collection of chairs, picnic table benches, and cushions was being set up on the grass by Margo, Nicky, and Claire. Kristy, who had an official Papadakis sitting job that evening, waved and came over with Sari on her hip and Andrew next to her. Mr. and Mrs. Pike had already claimed a picnic bench in the front row. Mr. Hobart walked through the gate, closing it behind him, and wandered over to claim an Adirondack chair next to the Pikes. Kids darted back and forth from behind the garage to the curtain.

Then Vanessa came out onto the stage. "Who knows what weirdness lurks in the hearts and minds of people and jerks," she chanted.

The tones of a Casio keyboard could be heard, punctuated by what sounded like the metal tops of saucepans clanging together. Kristy pointed, and Stacey realized that it was Marilyn, playing the opening theme. It sounded very good, but familiar. "The beginning of Beethoven's Fifth Symphony," explained Mallory, sliding in beside Kristy and Stacey. "That's what Marilyn told the triplets. That's their keyboard. Linny is playing the, ah, cymbals."

"Saucepan lids?" guessed Kristy.

Mallory nodded, grinning.

"I'm impressed," remarked Stacey. "How long has this been going on?"

"Ever since television got banned," answered Kristy. "All the kids have been in on it." She gave Stacey a reproachful look. "Haven't you been reading the club notebook? We've been writing about it."

"Shh," said Stacey, ducking the question. "They're about to begin."

Marilyn played some crashing chords on the keyboard, Vanessa bowed her way offstage, and the curtain swayed back.

Boo Hoo, Cassandra Clue had begun.

The curtain opened upon a terrible scene. Railroad tracks made out of scraps of lumber had been laid across the stage. Karen, who was Cassandra Clue, was tied across one of the tracks. The triplets, all wearing big moustaches and hats, strode out rubbing their hands.

"Ha," barked Adam. "Now you will never interfere with us again."

Byron made an elaborate show of picking up a dime off the track. "Completely flat," he announced, holding it up. "Not even enough left to make change. That's what the train is going to do to you, Clue."

"You'll never get away with this!" proclaimed Karen, struggling very convincingly against her bonds — so realistically that one hand popped free. Quickly she stuffed it back into place.

"HHHaaaahahahahaha," shouted Jordan, rubbing his hands together fiendishly.

"Did I miss anything?" gasped Claudia, sliding in next to Stacey.

"Nope," said Stacey. "You are just in the nick of time. I think the train is about to run over Cassandra Clue."

Offstage, Haley Braddock and Vanessa crooned, "Whooo, whoooo!"

"There's the train," snarled Jordan. "Good-bye forever, Clue."

The triplets dashed off.

"What will I do?" cried Cassandra. "Oh, where is Marvella?"

A chorus of voices offstage were chanting, "Choo, *choo*, choo, *choo*," punctuated by the Haley-Vanessa duo singing "Whoooo, whoo!" Faster and faster the sounds came.

Suddenly a cardboard train appeared at the far side of the stage, with Matt, Carolyn, and Nicky holding it up. They began to hop down the tracks toward Cassandra.

"Noooo!" screamed Cassandra.

The train kept coming. The train sounds got louder and faster.

Suddenly, Margo, wearing pointed ears and

a fuzzy tail, ran out toward Karen.

"It's Wonderwolf," cried Cassandra. "Quick, Wonderwolf! Bite through these ropes."

Wonderwolf cocked her head.

"The ropes," shouted Claire, from offstage.

"The ropes," said Cassandra quickly.

Wonderwolf knelt down beside the tracks. The train came closer. Closer.

Hannie ran up behind the train and saw what was happening. She clapped her hands to her face.

"Marvella!" cried Cassandra. "Help!"

The curtain swung shut just as Cassandra gave a horrifying scream.

"Will Wonderwolf save Cassandra in time? Or will she be flattened like a dime?" intoned Vanessa, strolling out onto the stage. "Stay tuned next week, same time, same place, for *Boo Hoo, Cassandra Clue.*"

Marilyn played some more Beethoven, accompanied by the crashing of cymbals.

The audience rose as one and gave the players a standing ovation.

"Wow," said Claudia. "That was excellent. Much better than television!"

Stacey said thoughtfully, "I don't think I've ever truly appreciated live theater, even when I was living in New York and going to Broadway shows, until now."

The cast came out and took several bows, applauding themselves and each other.

Then Mr. Pike announced, "We have lemonade and snacks ready for the cast and audience inside if someone will volunteer to help set up."

Naturally, there were plenty of volunteers. In no time at all, crew, cast, and audience were eating and drinking, and the cast and crew were arguing about the script for the next show.

Mal said, "I'm very much afraid that the train really wants to run over Cassandra."

Kristy laughed. "Don't worry. Karen will never let it happen."

"What happened to the diamonds?"asked Claudia, referring to the plot from last week.

"Stay tuned," said Mallory.

"Awesome," said Claudia. "Four stars and two thumbs up."

Mr. Braddock, who was pouring himself some lemonade, overheard Claudia's glowing review and laughed. "You know what's awesome?" he said. "We've let the kids start watching television again, albeit on a more limited basis. But I don't think they've even gone back to watching the real Cassandra Clue show. I think they like this better."

"What do you know?" remarked Kristy. "There *is* life after television."

CHAPTER 12

By Friday afternoon, half of Long Island had arrived in Stoneybrook.

Okay, I'm exaggerating. A little.

My father's father and mother, Grandfather David and Grandmother Ruth, and my mother's father and mother, Grandpa Morris and Gram (never Grandma!) Elsie were going to stay with us. The rest of our relatives were going to stay (to my relief) at the Strathmoore Inn. In fact, so many Stevensons, related by blood or marriage, had arrived that they had basically taken over the inn. That included my father's younger sister, Judith, who brought her children, five-year-old Sarah and four-year-old Lillian, and her husband, our uncle Saul; Aunt Esther and Uncle Mort, who are really our paternal great-aunt and -uncle, and who had come with their son Micah and his three kids, Aaron, Bette, and Jonathan, ages six, four, and two (his second wife, Janet, their mother, is a doctor, and was on call that weekend, and his teenage son Eli, who at seventeen-and-a-half was bored with Bat Mitzvahs and Bar Mitzvahs and all the rest, was visiting his mother in Baltimore); and my mother's first cousin, Jean, who had just gotten divorced. Cousin Jean had brought her two little kids, too: Amy and Sheila.

Our mother doesn't have any brothers or sisters. For this I was grateful. Seventeen people was enough.

Since our father's family is a big one, Anna and I had never been as close to Grandfather David and Grandmother Ruth as we had been to Grandpa Morris and Gram Elsie. We'd been especially close to Grandpa and Gram because Grandpa had been sick the year before we'd moved. He'd had triple bypass heart surgery, which had been really scary. He was better now, though still a little weak.

So we didn't quite knock him over when we threw our arms around him and Gram to welcome them.

I greeted everyone with hellos, then retreated to my room to worry about tomorrow.

Gram and Grandmother Ruth and Mom went into the kitchen, talking a hundred miles a minute about everything, from the caterers (Mom was cooking a feast for Friday night before we went for Shabbat services, but she had hired caterers for the Bat Mitzvah celebration in our backyard on Saturday night), to the tent (we were going to have a big white tent set up over part of the backyard), to whether Grandpa should be allowed to eat brisket — was it bad for his heart?

"Hey," I whispered out of the side of my mouth as Anna and I retreated up the stairs. "Where are the presents?"

"Abby! That's not what this is all about," Anna began, and then realized I was teasing her. It's not like Anna to be slow to catch on to even my feeblest jokes, which just shows that both of us were nervous.

"Let's start getting dressed for tonight," Anna suggested.

"Check," I said. I went to my room to wallow in nerves.

I'd pulled out my best dress (one of my only dresses, actually, except for the new dress that I'd just bought for the Bat Mitzvah party) and I was struggling with stockings when a brisk knock on my bedroom door was followed by Kristy saying, "Hey. Good grief! What are you hiding out in here for?"

"Don't be shy. Come on in," I replied. Kristy, of course, was already in my room, making herself at home.

Mary Anne stopped in the door and said, "Oh — you're getting dressed."

"Yeah." I shimmied into stockings. (Why are those things so hard to get on, anyway?)

Claudia appeared in the doorway. "You look very nice," she said.

"Your house is filling up with people," Mary Anne commented.

Sniffing the air, Claudia added, "And good smells."

"Mom's been cooking for days," I told her. "You should see the menu."

Just then Anna appeared in the doorway. "Hi, guys," she said.

Anna had on what she called one of her concert dresses: dark and plain, with little cap sleeves.

"Elegant," was Claudia's comment, and I had to agree.

As I finished getting ready, Kristy and Claudia told us about the show, *Boo Hoo, Cassandra Clue*, they'd seen that afternoon. And of course, Kristy brought me up to speed on the BSC meeting, which I'd missed.

We were all laughing as we went downstairs.

The house had filled up with people. I'd barely reached the bottom of the stairs before my uncle Mort had lifted me off the ground. "Is this my little girl?" he shouted. "Look at her!"

Anna got the same treatment. I made faces

at her over my uncle's shoulder. But we didn't mind. Uncle Mort and Aunt Esther are like that — enthusiastic. Even though they are our great-uncle and -aunt (our grandfather's sister and brother-in-law) and so much older, they seem to have more energy than, for instance, my father's brother-in-law, Saul. Uncle Saul is a lawyer, the kind of lawyer who never answers any question yes or no, and he frowns a lot and all his suits look exactly the same. Uncle Saul gave us all a dry handshake as I introduced my friends and explained that in honor of our Bat Mitzvah, they were donating free baby-sitting services for Shabbat.

Aunt Judith, who is our father's younger sister and is married to Uncle Saul, is nicer. She thanked Claudia, Kristy, and Mary Anne, and made a point of bringing over Sarah and Lillian, and introducing them. Although they weren't going to the synagogue that night, they were all dressed up in matching dresses with wide sashes, and white stockings with little flat shoes, and wore big bows in their hair. Sarah at five was behaving with careful dignity in her special clothes. Lillian at four was just excited, hopping up and down.

"We have to be very very careful not to spill," Sarah announced.

Claudia said, "Don't worry. We'll make sure you don't. And we'll have lots of fun tonight."

As Claudia led Lillian and Sarah toward the dining room, Aunt Judith said, "They can get out of their clothes and into their pj's once we leave. They'll be going to sleep soon after that."

We had to eat early, and Mom had set up everything buffet-style. It reminded me of the Thanksgiving dinner we prepared for all our families at Kristy's house, only not so big. But taking a cue from that dinner, Mom had set up a table in the dining room for the adults, and two smaller tables in the living room for the kids.

We worked our way down the buffet line and it was a feast: chicken, kugel, roast potatoes, roast carrots, challah . . . everything but dessert.

Dessert would come later, after synagogue.

Anna and I tried to slide into the tables with Kristy and Mary Anne and Claudia and the seven kids. Everyone was hitting it off great. We didn't really need three baby-sitters for seven kids, but it was easy to see that Kristy and Mary Anne and Claudia were having a fine time. Claudia was sitting with Lillian and Sarah and Jean's oldest daughter, Amy, who was also five and super adorable. Kristy was making a game out of putting Jonathan in his high chair. In honor of the occasion, Jonathan had on a long-sleeved shirt with a bow tie design at the neck. Mary Anne, Jonathan's brother, Aaron, his sister, Bette, and Amy's three-going-on-four sister, Sheila were all giggling about something. Aaron was dressed like a little adult, very cute in a suit with short pants. Bette wore a shiny skirt with a ruffle around the hem, and Sheila was wearing a pink dress with big white buttons down the front.

And of course, my friends had dressed up in their "good" baby-sitting clothes: Kristy had on cords instead of jeans, and was wearing a nice sweater over a button-down shirt. Mary Anne had on a pale yellow wool skirt, dark tights, a plaid vest, and a turtleneck sweater. Claudia had gone all out in a long skirt, lace socks peeking out above her black Doc Martens, and a tunic top with a belt she'd made herself out of twists of lace and a silver buckle. She wore her hair in a single braid tied with a piece of lace, and her earrings were silver snowflakes. Awesome as usual.

Who wouldn't want to sit with such an impressive-looking group?

But it was not to be. Grandma Ruth caught Anna and me and steered us gently back to the adult table.

"Tomorrow you take up your responsibilities as adults," she reminded us. "Tonight, you practice with us."

Anna and I sat.

It was fun. Our family hadn't been together like that for years. Not since Eli's Bar Mitzvah, I thought. Or was it when Micah and Janet had gotten married? No, before that. My father had been there, hadn't he?

Uncle Micah asked me a question about school and I got distracted, and before we knew it dinner was over. The evening passed quickly, like a dream. Soon all of the kids were asleep, tucked up in our bedrooms. We went to Friday night services and came home. Then Mom brought out Anna and Abby cakes for the guests, special desserts made in honor of our Bat Mitzvahs, like tiny, jewel-colored cupcakes with hard frosting. We ate the cakes and the grownups toasted us with wine and coffee and we drank soda and talked and talked and talked.

I watched my friends and family and felt proud. Shy Mary Anne was doing just fine with my cousin Jean, talking about Amy and Sheila. Kristy, used to large family gatherings, was moving confidently around the room from one conversation to another. Claudia had taken off her belt and I could tell by the gestures of her hand that she was explaining to my aunt Esther and uncle Mort how she'd made it. And I could tell they were impressed.

A hand touched my shoulder and I turned

to see Gram Elsie. Gram Elsie wears her hair short, just like my mother, but it is silver gray. Her eyes are so dark they almost seem black. And she is tiny. It is funny to watch her and Grandpa Morris, him towering above, his head bent slightly to one side, listening. Since he's been sick he's seemed stooped, smaller. But he's still taller than Gram.

"Hi," I said. "I don't think I'll ever get to sleep tonight."

Gram slid her hand down my arm to pat my hand. "You will, dear."

"I wish tonight could go on forever," I said impulsively. "Everyone together for always."

Gram patted my hand again. She looked both happy and sad. "It will," she assured me. "In your heart, you'll always remember."

A general movement had started toward the door. I joined my friends, my sister, and my mother in putting away Anna and Abby cakes for the children to have later, maybe with breakfast in the morning.

We hugged and kissed Gram and Grandpa, and Grandmother Ruth and Grandfather David, and went reluctantly up to bed. We left them downstairs, putting away dishes and laughing and talking.

I heard someone say my father's name, and a short silence. And then Grandfather David said, "Remember when he . . . "

And I heard my mother's laughter as Grand-father David finished talking.

Anna and I looked at each other and smiled.

"See you in the morning," I said.

And I went to bed and to my amazement, fell asleep almost instantly.

CHAPTER 13

I was nervous, nervous, nervous. So was Anna. Neither of us could eat breakfast. It was hard even to make coherent conversation with our grandparents.

We arrived at the synagogue early the next day and sat in the front row. Our relatives filed in behind us, along with other members of the congregation. Near the back, all in their BSC best, I saw my friends. Kristy gave me a thumbs-up signal, which might have made me smile if I hadn't been so nervous.

Then Rabbi Dorman began the service.

I don't remember much of it. It seemed to go by so quickly — and so slowly. I do recall the rabbi announcing our Bat Mitzvah. I remember folding and unfolding the piece of paper with my speech notes. Anna was clutching a piece of paper, too, but without moving. I recall the opening blessing. I remember standing up for the opening prayer.

Then suddenly it was time for the reading of the Torah. Rabbi Dorman turned and removed it from the Ark. The Ark is a special place where the Torah is kept. He brought out the Torah, which is written on a scroll of parchment, and handed it to Anna. Then I uncovered it and together we unrolled it reverently. The rabbi had told us that removing the Torah from the Ark symbolizes many things. And that when he handed the Torah to us, that was also symbolic. Anna and I were taking the laws of our people into our hands and becoming responsible for upholding them.

My sister and I joined the rabbi and the cantor. I don't remember how we got there. I listened to Anna chant. She seemed so clear and calm.

Then it was my turn to read from the Torah. I stepped up to where the Torah lay open, picked up the pointer to help me follow the text (the Torah is not supposed to be touched), and looked down. For a moment, I panicked. The symbols meant nothing. I was going to fail.

I looked out.

My family. All my family. I felt Anna's shoulder against mine.

I took a deep breath and began.

My voice didn't soar. But the words, so familiar now, with their familiar meanings, steadied me. The more I read, the more confident and calm I felt. I felt myself becoming part of the tradition, like my mother and father before me, my grandfathers before that. I paused and looked up and saw my grandmothers, nodding and smiling, and saw, too, the glisten of tears in Gram Elsie's eyes. My voice grew stronger. I was still shaky, but I wasn't afraid anymore.

After that, the Haftarah went really well. But there was still the sermon.

That's when Anna surprised me. She read a few lines from her Haftarah portion, then paused and said, "I was going to talk about my Torah portion. But I am not as good with words as I am with music. So, I'm going to let my music speak for me now."

She glanced at Rabbi Dorman, who nodded and smiled. Then she reached down beneath the podium and brought out her violin case. Lifting out the violin, she began to play.

It began simply and spread out, a shimmering shawl of sound. Then it drew back again, softer and softer. And then it was gone.

I was amazed. I had never heard my sister play like that before.

She put her violin down. Rabbi Dorman put one hand on my sister's shoulder and with the other, handed her a book. He nodded and spoke in a low voice and they both smiled.

I stepped forward. "Today I become an adult," I began. "A daughter of the commandment. I join a long tradition that includes not only my mother and father, my sister, my grandparents, but Jews all over the world and throughout the ages. Today, all over the world, other people my age join in these same readings from the Torah, and consider what it means to become a daughter — or son — of the commandment.

"In these past months of studying, I have learned my history, the history of my people. But it is my own history that I write with my actions. And I have learned, in this past week especially, the importance of every decision, large and small. How important it is to make the right decision. The true and truthful one."

I went on to talk, in general terms, about what had happened in the past week. The words came easily as I spoke, because I understood at last what I wanted to say and how to say it.

When I had finished, the rabbi said softly, "Well done, Abigail." He handed me a book, too, and I stroked the soft leather cover of it. "Thank you," I whispered.

I looked out. My mother was smiling. Gram's eyes had welled up with tears and she was touching her handkerchief to her eyes. In fact, all our grandparents looked teary-eyed.

But not me. I was proud and pleased and relieved and full of joy. The joy grew and grew in me as Rabbi Dorman stepped forward to speak.

He welcomed everyone to the Bat Mitzvah and to the synagogue. He continued, "And we welcome into our congregation two fine young women." He spoke of the passages we'd read from the Torah and its meaning to our lives and the lives of the Jewish community everywhere. He also said some nice things about us that made us giggle, but also made us feel good.

When he had finished he looked at each of us and used our Hebrew names. "*Hannah* and *Avigail*, terrific job. Your family, your friends, your congregation, and I are very proud of you. And you should be very proud of yourselves."

During the day, before our Bat Mitzvah party began, I opened some of the presents. Bonds for college from Aunt Judith and Uncle Saul and from Cousin Jean. A gold bracelet from Gram and Grandpa. Real, immediately spendable money from Aunt Esther and Uncle Mort. Pearl earrings from Cousin Micah and Cousin Janet. And a watch from Grandmother Ruth and Grandfather David.

Rabbi Dorman had given us each a book called *The Sabbath and Festival Prayer Book,* with an inscription. In mine he had written:

Congratulations

Abigail Stevenson

אבִיגֵיִל

on becoming a Bat Mitzvah

April 27 ‏אִיר 8

I really, really liked that. Then I remembered when I was little and my father told me what my Hebrew name meant. It means "father's light — his joy."

The most amazing gift of all was diamonds. Mom had taken her diamond earrings that Dad had given her and had each one set into a pendant on a gold chain.

I was speechless. Amazed. I hung the chain around my neck and felt the pendant rest against the pulse in my throat. Something from Mom — and from Dad.

And from the BSC? A gift certificate to the sporting goods store. A perfect gift.

It was finally time for the party to begin. It was a feast. Anna and I had chosen a joint theme. Can you guess what it was?

Soccer for me and music for Anna. Papier-mâché soccer balls and violins with purple balloons decorating every table. The large tent in our backyard looked amazing. At one end there was a colorful goal post hung with streamers. At the other end was a giant papier mâché violin, decorated with glitter. The napkins and tablecloths, some decorated with a sports motif and some with a musical one, were intermingled on the tables. Musical notes and soccer balls decorated the walls.

The dancing began right away while the DJ spun an interesting mix of traditional and non-traditional music. (With a lot of my favorite, Aretha Franklin, thrown in by special request.) I was dancing with my little cousin Aaron (actually we were both sort of hopping in place, and sometimes I was just swinging him around) when my grandpa Morris signaled the DJ. The next thing I knew, the whole room had swept into the Horah, a traditional circle dance at weddings and Bat and Bar Mitzvahs, with circles inside circles of people dancing in opposite directions. In the center, Anna and I were guided into chairs and lifted up and danced around.

It was a little like having your own parade, only better.

We got hugged a million times and said thank you a million times more, and yes, listened to all the embarrassing stories about our childhoods. The embarrassing stories (about flushing shoes down toilets and cutting our own hair and eating Play-Doh mixed with bananas) were an especially big hit with the little kids. But Claudia and Kristy and Stacey and Mary Anne and Logan and Shannon and Jessi and Mal were encouraging my aunts and uncles and grandparents, too.

I decided to forgive them all.

Then it was time to light the candles on the special cake: it was big and pink and as fancy as a wedding cake, with thirteen candles on it plus one for good luck. Anna and I had planned this part to be both serious and fun. As everyone grew quiet, Anna said, "The first candle is for our grandmothers, Grandmother Ruth — "

" — and Gram Elsie," I added. "We are happy they are able to celebrate our Bat Mitzvah with us."

"We'll always remember sleepovers at Grandmother Ruth's and her delicious chocolate brownies and, of course, her big bear hugs," said Anna.

"And we'll never forget, Gram Elsie, that you didn't punish us when we Magic Markered your living room walls. Thank you for your hilarious jokes and for loving us no matter what," I said. "We would like you both to come up and help us light our first candle."

Our grandmothers stood up and walked toward us. "Yea, Grandmother Ruth and Gram Elsie!" shouted Kristy, Stacey, and Claudia. After lighting the candle, my grandmothers showered us with hugs and kisses, and then returned to their seats. One by one we lit the candles honoring our family and friends, remembering both silly and serious things. Soon we came to candle eleven.

"This candle is for new friendship," I announced. "Would the members of the Babysitters Club please come forward? As so many clients have said before, I couldn't have made it without you." Anna asked her friends to come up too.

As our friends walked toward us I noticed Mallory and Mary Anne blushing furiously. Mary Anne stayed close to Logan, Kristy practically strutted, Jessi, Shannon, and Stacey stayed cool, and Claudia grinned. We all smiled for the camera as we lit the candle together.

Only three candles left after that. We thanked Mom for all she had done and lit the next candle with her.

"The next candle, candle number thirteen, is for our father," said Anna.

"Who is here with us today," I added.

We were silent for a moment, all of us remembering. Then Anna, my mother, and I lit the thirteenth candle.

Now there was one candle left. It was the candle for good luck.

"For Anna," I said.

"For Abby," she said.

"For our family," we said together.

And the photographer, who'd been lurking and flashing his camera, popped up again and blinded us with another flash.

And then the food. It was terrific. A lot of it was breakfast food (by special request) and all of it was delicious. We had chopped liver and pickled herring and lox and bagels, roast chicken, slices of tomato and cucumber, pickles and whitefish salad and lox salad, and for dessert, besides the cake, rugelach, an incredible little pastry rolled up with nuts and chocolate, and best of all, my mother's special chocolate babka, a truly amazing cake.

We ate and talked and played with the kids and I felt as if I were floating. I had made it. All those months of work and study had paid off. I felt grownup and like a giddy little kid at the same time.

Once again I found myself standing back to look at my friends, my family. And I thought of my father and knew that he would be pleased and proud. And because I was thinking of him, it was as if he were there.

We'd come a long way. A long way from Long Island to Stoneybrook. A great distance from the year our father had died, when the world had been such a bad place to live in.

I will miss my father always. But I could remember him, too. As if he were here. Now.

I had put my childhood behind me. But the world was a big place and full of all kinds of things, good and bad. I liked that, I decided. It gave me plenty of room to grow.

CHAPTER 14

Although we hadn't really planned it, we ended up having a sleepover after the party on Saturday night. Anna's friend Lauren from the orchestra stayed over, and Shannon, who had become friends with Anna, too, and every member of the BSC except Logan. We all crammed into our two rooms, and talked and talked and talked.

We made predictions about who we would be when we grew up. We wrote them down and folded them up and I put them in an old piggy bank, the kind you have to break to open.

"Okay," I intoned solemnly. "When we meet for our twentieth high school reunion —"

"Eww! No way I'll ever be that old!" shrieked Shannon.

"Our twentieth high school reunion," I repeated, "we'll open this and see if it came true."

"Excellent," said Claudia. "Are there any more of those Anna and Abby cakes left?"

We all laughed, and ate midnight snacks (and found Mom still up with our grandparents, talking over coffee in the kitchen). Then we played silly games such as gossip and truth or dare.

And the BSC presented me with one final, perfect gift: a memory glass filled with layers of salt and pepper like sand, and mementoes of the day; a bit of a streamer, a sprig of baby's breath from the flowers, a soccer napkin (clean) with everybody's name on it, my place card, and the melted friendship candle from the cake, all sealed with a melted soccer candle from one of the tables.

I could have stayed up all night, but slowly people began falling asleep, until only I was awake. I listened to Kristy shift and mumble in her sleeping bag on the floor, and heard a faint snore from somewhere else. I turned off my bedside light. A faint tracing of moonlight shone through the window.

I leaned over to look out. It was a clear, perfect night. Below, the white folds of the tent billowed slightly. Above, every star looked distinct and bright.

Suddenly I yawned so hard that my jaws cracked. What a long, strange trip it had been, I thought, remembering the Grateful Dead song that my mom liked so much.

I lay down on my bed and pulled up the covers. A long, strange trip. A good one.

So far.

I touched the necklace and fell asleep.

The caterers had done a massive cleanup job after the party. That meant we had plenty of room for creative breakfast-making the next morning. So we went for broke, from cereal to animal-shaped pancakes for the little kids who came over with their parents to say good-bye.

Aunt Judith and Uncle Saul left early, and stopped only long enough for Uncle Saul to fill his travel coffee mug.

Aunt Esther and Uncle Mort were going back with Grandfather David and Grandmother Ruth, so Cousin Micah dropped them off before he left with Aaron, Bette, and Jonathan. He was getting an early start, too.

Cousin Jean didn't have as far to go, so she stuck around for brunch, and helped us make funny-face pancakes for Amy and Sheila — and ourselves.

We all yawned a lot, grownups and baby-sitters. Then people began to slip away, one by one.

Gram and Grandpa were the last to go. I didn't want them to. I had a sudden rush of homesickness for Long Island. There, Gram and Grandpa hadn't been so far away.

I didn't like that they seemed smaller each time I saw them.

I hugged them both hard as if I could hold them there forever.

But in the end, I had to let them go.

We stood on the front steps, Anna and Mom and I, and waved good-bye. Then, in slow motion, we headed inside.

We spent the rest of the afternoon straightening up, looking over our gifts, and even writing a few thank-you notes.

I was glad to have something to keep me busy. I had a lot to think about, a lot to remember. But it was too soon.

By seven p.m., I was yawning hugely.

Don't tell anybody this, but by eight-thirty, I was in bed. Anna came in to sit by my feet. The diamond glinted on the chain around her neck.

"I'll never, ever forget this weekend," she said. "I wonder if someday I'll have a daughter and help her celebrate her Bat Mitzvah."

"It could happen," I said. Then I added,

"Wow, that would make me an aunt."

"Or you could have a daughter, too," Anna pointed out.

"Nah," I said, grinning. "Daughters are too much work."

We both laughed. Then Anna yawned, which made me yawn.

"Stop that," I ordered. "Don't you know yawning is contagious?"

"Then go to sleep," said Anna. "I'm going to." She got up. "Good night, Ms. Abigail Stevenson."

"Good night, Ms. Anna Stevenson," I answered.

I liked being called Ms. Being grown-up was going to be pretty decent, I decided. Maybe, as I had more practice at it, I wouldn't have such hard weeks, like the one before. Maybe, with practice, I could tell right away how to make the right decision and avoid the wrong one.

Looking back on everything that had happened, I felt older and wiser and more adult.

"Ms. Abigail Stevenson," I said aloud in the dark. "Ms. Abigail *Avigail* Stevenson." Then I grinned. "But you can call me Abby."

Dear Reader,

Abby's Lucky Thirteen is the second book narrated by our newest BSC member, Abby Stevenson. Abby is a lot of fun to write about because she's so passionate, and she's so different from the other club members. And I was also particularly happy to write about this very important time in her life, her Bat Mitzvah.

Although I like Abby's personality, I'm much more like her twin, Anna. Becoming a Bat Mitzvah is highly important to Anna, but she's terrified of giving a speech — one of the most important parts of the ceremony. I hate speaking in public, too. And I always thought that as I grew older it might become easier, but it never did. Even now when I'm on tour, I love meeting kids individually and signing books for them, but I never give talks. Stage fright has been such a big problem for me that I even wrote a book about it. And guess what the title is: *Stage Fright!*

Happy reading,

Ann M. Martin

Ann M. Martin

About the Author

ANN MATTHEWS MARTIN was born on August 12, 1955. She grew up in Princeton, NJ, with her parents and her younger sister, Jane.

Although Ann used to be a teacher and then an editor of children's books, she's now a full-time writer. She gets the ideas for her books from many different places. Some are based on personal experiences. Others are based on childhood memories and feelings. Many are written about contemporary problems or events.

All of Ann's characters, even the members of the Baby-sitters Club, are made up. (So is Stoneybrook.) But many of her characters are based on real people. Sometimes Ann names her characters after people she knows, other times she chooses names she likes.

In addition to the Baby-sitters Club books, Ann Martin has written many other books for children. Her favorite is *Ten Kids, No Pets* because she loves big families and she loves animals. Her favorite Baby-sitters Club book is *Kristy's Big Day*. (By the way, Kristy is her favorite baby-sitter!)

Ann M. Martin now lives in New York with her cats, Gussie and Woody. Her hobbies are reading, sewing, and needlework — especially making clothes for children.

Notebook Pages

This Baby-sitters Club book belongs to _____ .

I am _____ years old and in the _____

grade.

The name of my school is _____ .

I got this BSC book from _____ .

I started reading it on _____ and

finished reading it on _____ .

The place where I read most of this book is _____ .

My favorite part was when _____ .

If I could change anything in the story, it might be the part when

_____ .

My favorite character in the Baby-sitters Club is _____ .

The BSC member I am most like is _____

because _____ .

If I could write a Baby-sitters Club book it would be about ___

_____ .

#96 Abby's Lucky Thirteen

When Abby becomes a Bat Mitzvah, it's one of the most memorable moments of her life. The most memorable moment in my life (so far) was when _____ _____ . The second most memorable moment was when _____ _____ . Abby's Bat Mitzvah is something that is very important to her. Some things that are very important to me are _____ _____ . After the Bat Mitzvah ceremony, Abby's family throws a big party. The biggest party I ever attended was _____ _____ . Some of the people at this party were _____ _____ . If I were to throw a party right now, I would celebrate these things: _____ _____ . This is what my party invitation would look like.

Read all the books
about **Abby**
in the Baby-sitters Club series
by Ann M. Martin

#90 *Welcome to the BSC, Abby!*
No one said joining the Baby-sitters Club was
going to be easy!

#96 *Abby's Lucky Thirteen*
Abby's heading for big trouble on the biggest birthday of her life!

Mysteries:

#23 *Abby and the Secret Society*
Can Abby and the BSC solve an ugly mystery at
a beautiful country club?

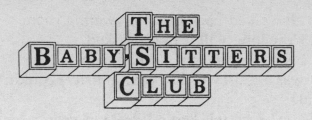

Look for #97

CLAUDIA AND THE WORLD'S
CUTEST BABY

I was halfway through the *American Medical Journal* when I heard a commotion near the nurse's desk. Then I thought I heard Peaches. Moaning.

I ran out to see two nurses wheeling Peaches, on a rolling bed, toward a pair of white, swinging doors. Russ was jogging alongside.

"Dr. Zuckerman to delivery, please," a voice blared over a loudspeaker. "Stat."

From behind us, a doctor walked briskly out of the maternity area. He ducked behind the nurses's desk, put on a shower cap and a green space suit, and went into the delivery room.

I squeezed Janine's hand. I felt as if I'd swallowed a beach ball.

"Come," Dad said. "Let's sit down."

He put his arm around Mom's shoulder, and

we all walked back into the waiting room.

"How long will it be?" I asked.

"Soon," Mom said. "Very soon."

I was a train wreck. I couldn't sit. I couldn't read.

Soon? *Soon* felt like a thousand years.

I thought Russ would never come. I thought he'd forgotten about us. I imagined us sitting there, neglected, gathering dust, until Little Mimi was ready for grade school.

And then, just when I thought I would pass out from the tension, Russ ran into the room. His eyes were glazed, his smile so bright we could have seen him in the dark.

"Claudia, Janine," he announced, "you have a new cousin."

The best friends you'll ever have!

Collect 'em all!

by Ann M. Martin

❏ MG43388-1	#1	Kristy's Great Idea	$3.50
❏ MG43387-3	#10	Logan Likes Mary Anne!	$3.99
❏ MG43717-8	#15	Little Miss Stoneybrook...and Dawn	$3.50
❏ MG43722-4	#20	Kristy and the Walking Disaster	$3.50
❏ MG43347-4	#25	Mary Anne and the Search for Tigger	$3.50
❏ MG42498-X	#30	Mary Anne and the Great Romance	$3.50
❏ MG42508-0	#35	Stacey and the Mystery of Stoneybrook	$3.50
❏ MG44082-9	#40	Claudia and the Middle School Mystery	$3.25
❏ MG43574-4	#45	Kristy and the Baby Parade	$3.50
❏ MG44969-9	#50	Dawn's Big Date	$3.50
❏ MG44968-0	#51	Stacey's Ex-Best Friend	$3.50
❏ MG44966-4	#52	Mary Anne + 2 Many Babies	$3.50
❏ MG44967-2	#53	Kristy for President	$3.25
❏ MG44965-6	#54	Mallory and the Dream Horse	$3.25
❏ MG44964-8	#55	Jessi's Gold Medal	$3.25
❏ MG45657-1	#56	Keep Out, Claudia!	$3.50
❏ MG45658-X	#57	Dawn Saves the Planet	$3.50
❏ MG45659-8	#58	Stacey's Choice	$3.50
❏ MG45660-1	#59	Mallory Hates Boys (and Gym)	$3.50
❏ MG45662-8	#60	Mary Anne's Makeover	$3.50
❏ MG45663-6	#61	Jessi's and the Awful Secret	$3.50
❏ MG45664-4	#62	Kristy and the Worst Kid Ever	$3.50
❏ MG45665-2	#63	Claudia's Special Friend	$3.50
❏ MG45666-0	#64	Dawn's Family Feud	$3.50
❏ MG45667-9	#65	Stacey's Big Crush	$3.50
❏ MG47004-3	#66	Maid Mary Anne	$3.50
❏ MG47005-1	#67	Dawn's Big Move	$3.50
❏ MG47006-X	#68	Jessi and the Bad Baby-sitter	$3.50
❏ MG47007-8	#69	Get Well Soon, Mallory!	$3.50
❏ MG47008-6	#70	Stacey and the Cheerleaders	$3.50
❏ MG47009-4	#71	Claudia and the Perfect Boy	$3.50
❏ MG47010-8	#72	Dawn and the We Love Kids Club	$3.50
❏ MG47011-6	#73	Mary Anne and Miss Priss	$3.50
❏ MG47012-4	#74	Kristy and the Copycat	$3.50
❏ MG47013-2	#75	Jessi's Horrible Prank	$3.50
❏ MG47014-0	#76	Stacey's Lie	$3.50
❏ MG48221-1	#77	Dawn and Whitney, Friends Forever	$3.50

More titles... ▶

The Baby-sitters Club titles continued...

❑ MG48222-X	#78	Claudia and the Crazy Peaches	$3.50
❑ MG48223-8	#79	Mary Anne Breaks the Rules	$3.50
❑ MG48224-6	#80	Mallory Pike, #1 Fan	$3.50
❑ MG48225-4	#81	Kristy and Mr. Mom	$3.50
❑ MG48226-2	#82	Jessi and the Troublemaker	$3.50
❑ MG48235-1	#83	Stacey vs. the BSC	$3.50
❑ MG48228-9	#84	Dawn and the School Spirit War	$3.50
❑ MG48236-X	#85	Claudi Kishli, Live from WSTO	$3.50
❑ MG48227-0	#86	Mary Anne and Camp BSC	$3.50
❑ MG48237-8	#87	Stacey and the Bad Girls	$3.50
❑ MG22872-2	#88	Farewell, Dawn	$3.50
❑ MG22873-0	#89	Kristy and the Dirty Diapers	$3.50
❑ MG22874-9	#90	Welcome to the BSC, Abby	$3.50
❑ MG22875-1	#91	Claudia and the First Thanksgiving	$3.50
❑ MG22876-5	#92	Mallory's Christmas Wish	$3.50
❑ MG22877-3	#93	Mary Anne and the Memory Garden	$3.99
❑ MG22878-1	#94	Stacey McGill, Super Sitter	$3.99
❑ MG45575-3		Logan's Story Special Edition Readers' Request	$3.25
❑ MG47118-X		Logan Bruno, Boy Baby-sitter Special Edition Readers' Request	$3.50
❑ MG47756-0		Shannon's Story Special Edition	$3.50
❑ MG47686-6		The Baby-sitters Club Guide to Baby-sitting	$3.25
❑ MG47314-X		The Baby-sitters Club Trivia and Puzzle Fun Book	$2.50
❑ MG48400-1		BSC Portrait Collection: Claudia's Book	$3.50
❑ MG22864-1		BSC Portrait Collection: Dawn's Book	$3.50
❑ MG48399-4		BSC Portrait Collection: Stacey's Book	$3.50
❑ MG47151-1		The Baby-sitters Club Chain Letter	$14.95
❑ MG48295-5		The Baby-sitters Club Secret Santa	$14.95
❑ MG45074-3		The Baby-sitters Club Notebook	$2.50
❑ MG44783-1		The Baby-sitters Club Postcard Book	$4.95

Available wherever you buy books...or use this order form.

Scholastic Inc., P.O. Box 7502, 2931 E. McCarty Street, Jefferson City, MO 65102

Please send me the books I have checked above. I am enclosing $_____
(please add $2.00 to cover shipping and handling). Send check or money order—no cash or
C.O.D.s please.

Name _____ Birthdate_____

Address _____

City_____ State/Zip _____

Please allow four to six weeks for delivery. Offer good in the U.S. only. Sorry, mail orders are not available
to residents of Canada. Prices subject to change.

BSC795

THE BABY-SITTERS CLUB®

Meet the best friends you'll ever have!

by Ann M. Martin

ALL NEW!

Have you heard? The BSC has a new look —and more great stuff than ever before. An all-new scrapbook for each book's narrator! A letter from Ann M. Martin! Fill-in pages to personalize your copy! Order today!

☐ BBD22473-5	#1	Kristy's Great Idea		$3.50
☐ BBD22763-7	#2	Claudia and the Phantom Phone Calls		$3.99
☐ BBD25158-9	#3	The Truth About Stacey		$3.99
☐ BBD25159-7	#4	Mary Anne Saves the Day		$3.50
☐ BBD25160-0	#5	Dawn and the Impossible Three		$3.50
☐ BBD25161-9	#6	Kristy's Big Day		$3.50
☐ BBD25162-7	#7	Claudia and Mean Janine		$3.50
☐ BBD25163-5	#8	Boy Crazy Stacey		$3.50
☐ BBD25164-3	#9	The Ghost at Dawn's House		$3.99
☐ BBD25165-1	#10	Logan Likes Mary Anne!		$3.99
☐ BBD25166-X	#11	Kristy and the Snobs		$3.99
☐ BBD25167-8	#12	Claudia and the New Girl		$3.99

Available wherever you buy books, or use this order form.

Send orders to Scholastic Inc., P.O. Box 7500, 2931 East McCarty Street, Jefferson City, MO 65102.

Please send me the books I have checked above. I am enclosing $_____ (please add $2.00 to cover shipping and handling). Send check or money order—no cash or C.O.D.s please.

Please allow four to six weeks for delivery. Offer good in the U.S.A. only. Sorry, mail orders are not available to residents in Canada. Prices subject to change.

Name_____ Birthdate ___/___/___
First   Last   D / M / Y
Address_____

City_____ State_____ Zip_____

Telephone (___) _____   ☐ Boy   ☐ Girl

Where did you buy this book? Bookstore ☐   Book Fair ☐
                              Book Club ☐   Other ☐

SCHOLASTIC

BSCE995

THE BABY-SITTERS CLUB®

by Ann M. Martin

Collect and read these exciting BSC Super Specials, Mysteries, and Super Mysteries along with your favorite Baby-sitters Club books!

BSC Super Specials

❑ BBK44240-6	Baby-sitters on Board! Super Special #1	$3.95
❑ BBK44239-2	Baby-sitters' Summer Vacation Super Special #2	$3.95
❑ BBK43973-1	Baby-sitters' Winter Vacation Super Special #3	$3.95
❑ BBK42493-9	Baby-sitters' Island Adventure Super Special #4	$3.95
❑ BBK43575-2	California Girls! Super Special #5	$3.95
❑ BBK43576-0	New York, New York! Super Special #6	$3.95
❑ BBK44963-X	Snowbound! Super Special #7	$3.95
❑ BBK44962-X	Baby-sitters at Shadow Lake Super Special #8	$3.95
❑ BBK45661-X	Starring The Baby-sitters Club! Super Special #9	$3.95
❑ BBK45674-1	Sea City, Here We Come! Super Special #10	$3.95
❑ BBK47015-9	The Baby-sitters Remember Super Special #11	$3.95
❑ BBK48308-0	Here Come the Bridesmaids! Super Special #12	$3.95

BSC Mysteries

❑ BAI44084-5	#1 Stacey and the Missing Ring	$3.50
❑ BAI44085-3	#2 Beware Dawn!	$3.50
❑ BAI44799-8	#3 Mallory and the Ghost Cat	$3.50
❑ BAI44800-5	#4 Kristy and the Missing Child	$3.50
❑ BAI44801-3	#5 Mary Anne and the Secret in the Attic	$3.50
❑ BAI44961-3	#6 The Mystery at Claudia's House	$3.50
❑ BAI44960-5	#7 Dawn and the Disappearing Dogs	$3.50
❑ BAI44959-1	#8 Jessi and the Jewel Thieves	$3.50
❑ BAI44958-3	#9 Kristy and the Haunted Mansion	$3.50

More titles ➡

The Baby-sitters Club books continued...

❏ BAI45696-2	#10 Stacey and the Mystery Money	$3.50
❏ BAI47049-3	#11 Claudia and the Mystery at the Museum	$3.50
❏ BAI47050-7	#12 Dawn and the Surfer Ghost	$3.50
❏ BAI47051-5	#13 Mary Anne and the Library Mystery	$3.50
❏ BAI47052-3	#14 Stacey and the Mystery at the Mall	$3.50
❏ BAI47053-1	#15 Kristy and the Vampires	$3.50
❏ BAI47054-X	#16 Claudia and the Clue in the Photograph	$3.50
❏ BAI48232-7	#17 Dawn and the Halloween Mystery	$3.50
❏ BAI48233-5	#18 Stacey and the Mystery at the Empty House	$3.50
❏ BAI48234-3	#19 Kristy and the Missing Fortune	$3.50
❏ BAI48309-9	#20 Mary Anne and the Zoo Mystery	$3.50
❏ BAI48310-2	#21 Claudia and the Recipe for Danger	$3.50
❏ BAI22866-8	#22 Stacey and the Haunted Masquerade	$3.50
❏ BAI22867-6	#23 Abby and the Secret Society	$3.99

BSC Super Mysteries

❏ BAI48311-0	The Baby-sitters' Haunted House Super Mystery #1	$3.99
❏ BAI22871-4	Baby-sitters Beware Super Mystery #2	$3.99

Available wherever you buy books...or use this order form.

Scholastic Inc., P.O. Box 7502, 2931 East McCarty Street, Jefferson City, MO 65102-7502

Please send me the books I have checked above. I am enclosing $ _____
(please add $2.00 to cover shipping and handling). Send check or money order
— no cash or C.O.D.s please.

Name_____Birthdate_____

Address _____

City_____State/Zip_____

Please allow four to six weeks for delivery. Offer good in the U.S. only. Sorry, mail orders are not
available to residents of Canada. Prices subject to change.

BSCM795

"Wonderful Family Entertainment!"

– Pam Thomson, KABC-TV

The First Baby-Sitters Club Full-Feature Film
Based On Scholastic's Best Selling Book Series By Ann M. Martin

NOW AVAILABLE FOR SALE WHEREVER VIDEOS ARE SOLD!

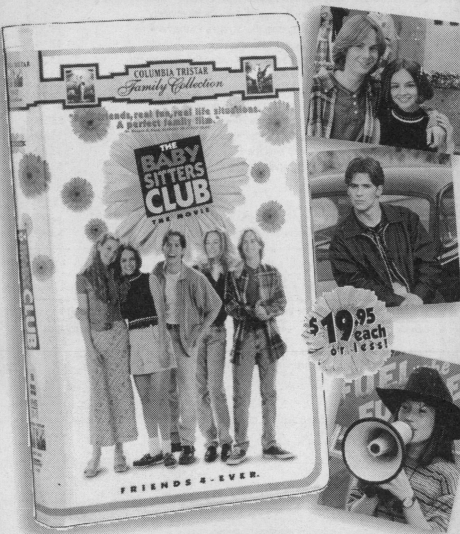

Also Available on Laserdisc and VHS Slip-sleeve.

BEACON and COLUMBIA PICTURES PRESENT A SCHOLASTIC PRODUCTION "THE BABY-SITTERS CLUB" MUSIC BY DAVID MICHAEL FRANK CO-PRODUCED BY TINA STERN EXECUTIVE PRODUCERS MARC ABRAHAM, THOMAS A. BLISS, MARTIN KEITZ, DEBORAH FORTE BASED ON THE BOOK SERIES BY ANN M. MARTIN WRITTEN BY DALENE YOUNG PRODUCED BY JANE STARTZ AND PETER O. ALMOND DIRECTED BY MELANIE MAYRON

COLUMBIA PICTURES

© 1995 COLUMBIA PICTURES INDUSTRIES, INC. ALL RIGHTS RESERVED.   © 1995 LAYOUT AND DESIGN COLUMBIA TRISTAR HOME VIDEO. ALL RIGHTS RESERVED.   DISTRIBUTED THROUGH SONY PICTURES RELEASING